Home Is Where Your Heart Is

(Home To You Series #2)

Morris Fenris

Home Is Where Your Heart Is
Home To You Series #2

Table of Contents

Prologue 5

Chapter 1 11

Chapter 2 19

Chapter 3 25

Chapter 4 31

Chapter 5 38

Chapter 6 46

Chapter 7 54

Chapter 8 62

Chapter 9 67

Chapter 10 71

Chapter 11 78

Chapter 12 85

Chapter 13 92

Chapter 14 97

Chapter 15 102

Chapter 16 108

Chapter 17 113

Chapter 18 120

Chapter 19 124

Chapter 20 128

Chapter 21 136

Chapter 22 143

Chapter 23 149

Chapter 24 153

Chapter 25 157

Chapter 26 162

Chapter 27 166

Epilogue..170

Sample of Book 3 174

Thank You 183

Prologue

Six years earlier,

San Francisco, California...

Jessica felt the bed dip beneath Dino's weight and kept her eyes shut, hoping he'd think she was still asleep and leave her alone. The last three weeks of her life had been a rollercoaster of emotions, ranging from happiness to sheer terror. She was currently teetering on the edge of terror and needed some time to talk herself down off the ledge before she had to interact with Dino or any of his thugs. Three years ago, Dino had introduced Sam, Jimmy, and Tony to her as his friends. She now knew differently.

"Baby, you awake?" Dino's voice came from right above her shoulder. Jessica held herself still, but left her body relaxed. She did her best to keep her breathing nice and even, but her heart was already picking up speed and she could only pray that Dino would believe her ruse and leave the room before she gave herself away.

"I tired you out, didn't I? Well, that's okay. I've got some business to take care of in town. Sleep and when I get back, we'll talk about your new role. I know I scared you, but it was for your own good. Things are going to be better than ever, you'll see."

Jessica felt his weight leave the mattress and a moment later the bedroom door shut, and she heard the sound of the key turning in the lock. She waited for a count of thirty before she hesitantly opened her eyes, her left one only partially opening due to the swelling and bruising. She couldn't say for sure whose fist had caused the most damage and the fact that she even had to think about such a thing told her just how much trouble she'd landed herself in.

She carefully rolled over to her back and saw that she was indeed alone in the room. She forced herself to get out of the bed, ignoring the aching in her arms and the bruising already visible around her wrists. Dino had been less than pleased when he'd come home early and found her packing her suitcases. Jessica had hoped to be long gone before he arrived, but she'd misjudged the time and her clean getaway had gone awry.

Three weeks earlier, Dino had wined and dined her and played upon the teenage infatuation Jessica had developed for him three years earlier when he'd rescued her from living on the streets. She'd placed Dino on a pedestal and on her seventeenth birthday, when he'd proposed they take their relationship beyond friendship, Jessica's heart had been overflowing with happiness. She'd immediately agreed and for three weeks, she'd been living in a little dream world where Dino Salvatori eventually married her and they lived happily ever after. Jessica now knew that was only a pipe dream and one that she would never experience as long as Dino was in the picture.

Dino, his brother, and his father were businessmen, but until a few days ago, Jessica had been unaware of exactly what they were selling that earned them so much money. The lavish lifestyle he'd exposed her to was merely a smoke screen for the depravity that fueled his family's bank accounts. She'd suspected for a while now that Dino might be dealing in black market merchandise or even some gateway drugs like marijuana; she'd never imagined how wrong she was. Not until she'd shown up at his father's distribution center to surprise him with a late picnic lunch and interrupted him unloading the back of a cargo trailer.

She'd been about to call out to him when the door had opened and a young woman had toppled to the ground with a sharp cry of pain. Dino's thugs had climbed into the truck and Jessica had watched in stunned disbelief as eight more teenage girls were removed from the trailer, each with their hands shackled behind their backs and tears streaming down their faces. She'd not known what to do and while she'd stood there watching, Tony had interrogated each girl as to her name and age. Failure to answer him quickly enough had resulted in them receiving the back of his hand across their faces.

Jessica had wanted to cry out for him to stop, but as she moved to step forward, a forklift came around the tractor trailer and two pallets of material were unloaded. Dino used his pocket knife to remove a white brick of something from one of the pallets and then he poked the package with it and white powder spilled out. Dino dipped his pinky finger into the substance and tasted it, shaking his head and pronouncing it acceptable.

At that point, Jessica had seen way more than she wanted to and she backtracked, keeping her eyes on the scene before her until she was safely around the corner of the main building, wherein, she turned and hurried to her vehicle. She drove straight home, her emotions all over the place. She felt betrayed and stupid for not having seen what was going on sooner.

Once back at their apartment, she began filling suitcases with her clothing and other belongings. She'd already check out the bus schedule and she planned to be on it before the sun went down, but Dino had come home early. He'd been furious that she had shown up at the warehouse and Jessica's temper had flared and all of the questions racing through her mind had come tumbling out.

Who were those girls? Why were their hands tied behind their back? What was that white powder?

She'd not seen the change in Dino until it was too late. He'd been coldly furious and yet, he'd answered every one of her questions. In more detail than she cared for. When Jessica expressed her outrage, Dino had merely laughed and told her to get used to it as he wasn't letting her go. She'd unleashed her anger on him, which, looking back now, had been a major mistake. Dino had retaliated in kind, slapping her so hard she lost her footing and then locking her in their bedroom with the threat that if she didn't watch her manners and show some gratitude, he'd be more than willing to let Sam, Jimmy and Tony try teaching her some.

As threats went, Dino had known how she would respond to his words. All of the fight had left her and she'd been more than willing to appease Dino in any way he chose to avoid being passed around to his thugs as a play thing. Any trust of feelings she'd had for Dino had been obliterated in that moment and she'd been plotting for a way to get away from him for the last forty-eight hours. Now that the time had come, she only hoped she could pull it off. Failure would come at way too high of a price.

She located the screwdriver she'd swiped from the toolbox after Tony had been summoned to fix the bathroom sink that was leaking. She'd loosened the pipes herself, and while Tony had been making the necessary repairs, she'd grabbed the screwdriver and shoved it between the mattresses. He'd not missed it, nor had he come looking for it.

She listened at the door, smiling when she heard nothing. The first day she'd been locked inside, she'd been able to hear Sam, Jimmy, and Tony keeping guard outside the door. Not today, though. She knocked on the door, calling for anyone who could hear her but only silence remained.

She used the screwdriver to pop the hinge pins on the door and then carefully pulled it towards her and then slid it to the left until the locking mechanism released and the door practically fell on top of her. She settled it against the wall, reached underneath the bed for the pillow case she'd filled with some extra clothing and the cash she'd been saving up, and she headed for the patio door.

A fire escape ladder could be extended all the way to the alley below, and Jessica wasted no time in forcing it to deploy and making her way down the metal stairs. Once on the street level, she headed for the end of the alley, only to duck back just in time to avoid being seen by Tony as he stood guard by the entrance.

Jessica retraced her steps and headed for the women's shelter located a few blocks south of her current position. Half an hour later and more than one pep talk for courage held, she stepped through the doors of a women's shelter, shaking like a leaf in the thin jacket and leggings she'd donned before tackling the door hinges. The director of the facility had been very kind to her and had insisted that Jessica visit with their resident nurse for a few minutes before she was asked to fill out some paperwork.

Jessica had done so, allowing the nurse to examine her bruises, bandage the worst ones, and take down some basic information. The nurse had performed a routine pregnancy test and Jessica had been stunned to find out it was positive. She'd cried for almost an hour on the nurse's shoulder before the director had been summoned and Jessica had been pressed for Dino's last name. She'd finally relented and given it only to see shock and disbelief on the director and nurse's faces. Jessica had still been trying to come to terms with the idea that in nine months she was going to be a mother and had missed the director excusing herself to make a phone call.

When Jessica had finally pulled herself together and headed back to the common room, it was to see Dino and Tony stepping through the front doors. Dino had greeted the facility director very warmly and it was obvious that they were old friends. Jessica's hope had been shattered and she'd bolted for the nearest exit. She'd left behind her extra clothes and everything not already on her person, her only thoughts were those of protecting her unborn child and keeping him safe from Dino and his illegal activities.

She'd been carrying around her cash since arriving at the shelter, not trusting that someone else wouldn't go through her belongings when she wasn't with them and abscond with it. She purchased a one-way bus ticket on the first bus out of town and ended up somewhere in Oregon by nightfall. She slept on a bench and the next morning she bought another one-way ticket. She continued to do this until she ended up in Washington State, almost out of funds and tired of feeling like throwing up the entire bus ride. Seattle hadn't been the most inviting place in the world, but no one knew her there and it was as good as a place as any to start putting down roots. Or so she'd thought.

Being pregnant, seventeen, and living on the street in a city situated next to the ocean had been less than desirable and surviving had become harder and harder. So had staying ahead of Dino and his network of like-minded criminals. Dino had issued a hefty reward for information about her current location and the same people who offered to share their fires at night had also been the first ones to rat her out.

Before she'd reached her third trimester, she'd been on the run again. She'd taken buses or hitchhiked, eventually winding up in Utah just before she was to give birth. She found a shelter there who offered her a safe haven to have her baby in and she'd remained there for three months. Then she'd seen a flyer with her picture on it lying in the street where the homeless kids hung out. Dino hadn't given up on her and Jessica had panicked again.

She'd loaded up baby Zane and started moving around once more, never staying in one place longer than a few weeks to a month. Until she'd landed in Cheyenne. She'd arrived there with a sick little boy and had been forced to seek help from the local social services people. That's where her life had seemed to take a turn for the better.

Chapter 1

Thursday, January 10th,

Cheyenne, Wyoming...

Rylor Ballard stacked the court records neatly and then paper clipped them together before tossing them onto the pile of paperwork needing to be filed away. Today was the last day of his work week and he was more than ready for a few days off. So far this week, he'd testified in a court proceeding removing two children from the custody of their abusive and neglectful parents. He'd also been present at a video hearing for a fifteen-year-old who had threatened to beat up one of his teachers. The young man's parents were refusing to let him come home and Rylor had recommended he be sent to the state juvenile detention facility in Laramie. He'd be able to get some counseling for his anger management issues there and still work towards completing his high school graduation requirements.

He picked up a pen and signed the stack of papers one of the secretaries had set on his desk while he was out to lunch.

"Sherry, these are ready to go over to the courthouse. Don't forget I'm gone tomorrow and most of next week."

"I remember. That guy from the FBI called, he wants to set up a meeting for next Wednesday. Will you be back by then?"

"I'll make it a point to be. Go ahead and call him back and schedule it for mid-morning. I may wait and drive in Wednesday morning depending on the weather."

"When are you leaving for your sister's wedding?"

11

"Tomorrow as soon as I pick her up at the airport. She's been in Nashville recording her first solo album."

"I can't wait to hear it. Jerricha's voice is so smooth and peaceful."

"I'll pass along the compliment."

The sound of his phone ringing sent him back into his office. He took a seat behind the desk and rolled his tense shoulders a bit and then absently picked up the ringing phone next to his elbow.

"Rylor Ballard."

"Mr. Ballard, this is Mike down at security. I need you to come down here for a moment. You have a visitor, er... make that two visitors."

Rylor gave the phone a puzzled look and then dropped the pen in his hand down onto the desk and headed for the stairs. He could have taken the elevator but whenever possible, Rylor liked to combine his workday with a bit more exercise than was required to sit behind a desk or in a courtroom.

He reached the main lobby and immediately saw Jessica Niles, known to him as Jessie, trying to contain her five-year old son, Zane. She was wearing torn jeans and the polo shirt with the convenience store logo stitched on the upper left chest. Her hair was coming out of the haphazard ponytail and she looked agitated, even from a distance.

Rylor headed across the foyer, watching Zane try to figure out how to climb up onto the retaining wall of the indoor terrarium. It was three feet tall and Zane was doing very well at trying to get his feet up on top of it.

"Sweetheart, don't climb on that. Rylor will be coming out to see us real soon. I promise."

Rylor smiled at the happiness that spread over Zane's face

12

and quickened his step, wondering what had put that frightened look in Jessie's eyes. He'd first met her six months earlier when he'd been called to the after-hours urgent care clinic. Jessie had arrived in Cheyenne by bus with a very sick toddler in tow. Zane had been running a fever over one hundred and two and had been diagnosed with influenza. Jessie had tearfully told him she had no place to go and couldn't afford to rent a hotel room and still feed the both of them. She'd been terrified that Rylor was there to take her son away from her. That had been the furthest thing from his mind and he'd done everything in his power to convince her of that fact.

Rylor had immediately arranged for her to receive a temporary housing subsidy and had seen to it that she was given a room at the halfway house for single mothers. Jessie had been very grateful and over the course of the next several months, Rylor had been able to help her put her life back together. As a social worker for the great state of Wyoming, and the first point of contact she'd had, Rylor had been assigned her case. He'd requested her records from California and then promptly discarded the thin file that told him nothing of value. Instead, he spent a good amount of time with Jessie, getting to know her and developing his own opinion of her character.

He'd helped her sign up for classes designed to help her attain her GED, applauded as she walked across the stage to accept her certificate, and treated her and Zane to pizza and milkshakes afterward. He'd written a letter of recommendation to the local technical school that had helped her get accepted, and aside from their mandated weekly progress meetings, he'd become her one and only friend. He'd come close to breaking department policy by becoming too involved with her and her son, but he'd been unable to help himself. Jessie needed someone to believe in her while she healed enough to believe in herself. That was Rylor's specialty.

Zane saw him when he was still a dozen feet away and launched himself across the slippery floor, "Rylor!"

13

Rylor swept him up in his arms at the same time his little feet slipped, and he threw his arms out. "Whoa there, little man. What's the hurry?"

"Mama said I's gets to come see you," Zane told him with a happy grin.

Rylor nodded and then met Jessie's frightened eyes, "What's going on?"

Jessie wrung her hands and then glanced at the security guard who was watching them intently. "Can I talk to you for a minute?"

Rylor nodded and gestured towards one of the small sitting areas on the other side of the large foyer. "Sure." He chose an area with a small child's play block and took a moment to get Zane interested in the toy, giving him and Jessie a chance to talk quietly without interruption.

"Tell me what's going on. You look scared."

Jessie shook her head, "I need to take care of something and I may need to leave town."

Rylor shook his head and then asked, "You need to leave town? Where are you going?"

"That doesn't matter, but I can't take Zane with me. Rylor, I know it's not in your job description, but I really need you to watch him for me."

"Jessie, back up a minute. How long are you going to be gone?"

"I can't tell you any more, I just need you to watch him. Please? It's really important to me that I know he's safe."

"Why wouldn't he be safe?" Rylor asked, red flags popping up all over.

"I promise to explain things when I can... please, can I leave him here with you? I need to go."

Rylor watched her with narrowed eyes as she glanced at the street, tension evident in her shoulders and the stiff way she held her spine. "Jessie, talk to me. What's going on?"

"Rylor, I can't. Please... it's a matter of life or death. Keep Zane safe for me. Just for tonight."

"Jessie, you know my sister's getting married Sunday. I'm supposed to leave for Warm Springs tomorrow afternoon."

"Hopefully this won't take too long, and I'll be back for Zane tonight, or first thing in the morning."

Rylor searched her eyes and then asked once more, "Sure you won't tell me what's going on?"

Jessie shook her head and then gave him a tight smile. 'Thank you." She walked over and enfolded Zane in a big hug, kissing his cheek and then telling him, "You're going to have a sleepover with Rylor. Okay?"

Zane looked at Rylor and then nodded, "Okay."

Jessie nodded and Rylor could tell she was holding back tears as she released him and stood up. She glanced his direction and he took a step back, gesturing for her to follow him. "Whatever this is about, you know I only want to help."

"I know that, but this is something I have to do. Please understand," she begged him.

"I'll try. Be safe," Rylor told her, not sure why he felt the need to do so.

"Here are his things. I... he's the only thing I have. Please keep him safe."

"Of course, I'll keep him safe. I'll keep you safe, too. Jessie, if you're in some sort of trouble, talk to me. I want to help you."

Jessie gave him a tired smile and then walked close and kissed his cheek, "I know you do but you can't help me with this. It's something I have to do."

Rylor watched her, wondering if she was ever going to trust him enough to share her past with him. He knew a few details of her life, starting with her time in the California foster care system and ending up with her having to leave California in a hurry. He knew she wasn't wanted by the authorities for anything, but beyond that, he didn't know anything concrete. Knowing he wasn't going to get anything more from her right now, he finally sighed and nodded, "You're going to explain everything to me when you get back. And I do mean everything. All of it. California. Zane. You're not going to leave anything out if I do this for you. Got it?"

Jessie gave him the first real smile and nodded, "I promise I'll do that."

"Remember that address I gave you," Rylor reminded her. "That's where I'm going when you get back. If you ever need a safe place to go, Warm Springs is there for you. Just ask anyone in the town for the Ballard family. They'll get ahold of my parents or siblings to keep you safe until I can get there. Promise me?" Rylor demanded, alarm bells still going off inside his head.

"I remember. I've got to go," Jessie told him, taking one last look at Zane and then heading quickly for the door and the winter weather outside.

"Well, at least she has a coat on." Rylor murmured to himself, always amazed that Jessie didn't dress more appropriately for the weather. In the beginning, her lack of proper clothing had been due to her deficient wardrobe. Now, however, it was just due to lack of foresight. Sighing, he turned to Zane and then held out his arms as he squatted down to the little boy's level. "Hey, buddy. Want to go help me clean up my office?"

Zane ran into his arms and nodded, "I'm a good helper, mama says so."

"Good, because I'm kind of a messy person. According to my family, I need all of the help I can get." Rylor opted to take the elevator back up and soon he and Zane were making good headway on clearing off his desk. Rylor might be messy while working, but he was a stickler for leaving a clean desk at the end of the workday. With him planning to be gone for several days, he wanted nothing sitting on his desk when he left today.

"Sherry, these files all need to be put away." He handed the stack of file folders off to her. "Did you get ahold of Trevor?"

"I did. He and his partner will be here at 10:30 Wednesday morning."

"Very good," Rylor went back into his office. His only sister was getting married to the principal of the secondary school in Warm Springs and since he hadn't been home in several months, Rylor was looking forward to it. He had requested several additional days off, but where he would spend them all with his family remained to be seen. He had a telephone conference call set up for Monday and that would determine how the rest of his week progressed.

For tonight however, he and a little five-year old had a date with a pizza and the latest cartoon movie. "Zane, are you ready to go?"

"Where are we going?" Zane asked, grabbing his hand as they left his office and headed for the elevator.

"How does pizza sound?" Rylor asked.

"Can we get the cookie stuff, too?" Zane asked, bouncing up and down as the elevator moved downward.

"I think we can do that." Rylor had a sweet tooth and so did little Zane. "I think I even have some ice cream in the freezer we can have with them."

"Yay!" Zane jumped up and down as the elevator stopped and the doors opened.

Rylor grinned at the security guard and then swept Rylor up into his arms. "Let's get this party started then."

Chapter 2

Leaving Zane with Rylor was one of the hardest things Jessie had done in a long while. Not because she didn't trust Rylor or hadn't left him for short periods of time before, but the reason behind her leaving him was one that terrified her. She stood outside the State Department building and watched until he and Zane got on the elevator. Only then did she remember the scare she'd had an hour earlier.

Jessie had been tending the cash register in a small gas station located at the edge of town and right off the highway. It wasn't her normal shift, but she never turned down hours if at all possible. It helped that the owner didn't mind Zane tagging along and playing in the office behind the cashier's area. As jobs went, it wasn't exciting and only paid twenty-five cents above minimum wage, but it was a job and helped put food in their mouths.

Jessie had just been finishing up her last sale and had been looking forward to getting back to her small studio apartment when a dark colored suburban had pulled up in front of the pumps. Everything was automated and when the buzzer had gone off alerting the cashiers to the fact that someone was making a credit card purchase outside, neither she nor her co-worker had paid much mind.

"Thanks for covering part of my shift," Stacy told her with a smile.

"No problem. Classes don't start again until next week and Zane and I weren't doing much."

"He sure is a cutie."

Jessie agreed and headed for the office. She was packing up Zane's toys when a voice from her past had the blood in her veins running cold.

"Miss, I was wondering if I might trouble you for some information."

Jessie's heart was in her lungs as she gingerly pushed the office door most of the way closed. There was a mirror on her boss's back wall and she positioned herself to where she could see the image of the man at the counter. She covered her mouth with a hand to contain her gasp of fear when Tony's face appeared.

"Oh no," she whispered brokenly. Her heart was racing and all she could think of was that somehow he'd found her.

"We're looking for a friend of ours and think she might be living here. This is her picture. Could you see of you recognize her?"

Jessie stopped breathing and waited for her co-worker to rat her out. She saw Stacy meet her eyes in the mirror that only employees would know was in the office and Jessie watched her lie to Tony.

"That doesn't look like anyone I've seen. Who is she? Someone famous?"

Tony smiled and shook his head, handing Stacy a business card. "If you do happen to see her, give this number a call. It's really important that we find her."

"I'll do that. Anything else I can do for you?" Stacy asked.

"No, just the map. Thanks."

"No problem. That'll be $7.52."

Dino had entered the store by this time and he handed Stacy some money, "No luck?"

"None," Tony replied. "Thanks again."

"Sure. You guys have a good day," Stacy told them with a flirty little wave. *If she only knew what those men were capable of.*

Jessie remained frozen until Dino and Tony had left the inside of the store. Only then did Jessie move. She packed Zane's things up and picked him up, shushing him when he started to whine in protest that he wasn't done playing yet.

"You can play later," she told him. Her mind was frantic and suddenly she knew where she needed to go. Zane needed to be somewhere safe and the only person she trusted to ensure that was Rylor. She left the small office and gave Stacy a tight smile, "Thanks for that."

"Sure. Did you see that hottie that was just in here? The plates are from California… why don't guys who look like that live in Wyoming? And why are they searching for someone who looks just like you?" Stacy asked.

Jessie shook her head, "Stacy, looks aren't everything. In fact, in my experience, guys who look like that are really the scum of the earth. Not anyone you want to get mixed up with. Trust me on this. I'm going to get Zane out of here. If they come back, just… well, be careful. Okay?"

Stacy shrugged her shoulders, "Whatever. It's not like they're sticking around town. He said they were looking for a friend and thought she might have come through here. They wanted directions to the bus station."

Jessie felt like crying but held it together a few moments longer. She made sure the suburban was nowhere to be seen before stepping outside with Zane in tow. She headed for the nearest bus stop and was relieved when she only had to wait a minute before it arrived.

Somehow, her past had managed to catch up with her and the life she was starting to build here was now in jeopardy. The difference between now and six years ago was vast. Since arriving in Cheyenne, Jessie had somehow regained her self-confidence and the fight that had kept her alive for so many years without a place to call home or people who actually cared about her. That indomitable spirit was alive and well and she was not going to hand over her life in Cheyenne without knowing there was no other choice.

"Zane, how would you like to go see if Rylor wants to play?"

Zane adored Rylor and Jessie seconded the feeling. But not in the way everyone who saw them together believed. Rylor was the knight-in-shining-armor and big brother she never had, all rolled into one handsome man who had befriended her when she was at her lowest. Rylor had made it possible for her to actually believe she could put down roots and make a life and family for herself. Dino didn't get to take that away. Not now. Not without a fight.

Jessie shook her head, pulling her mind back to the present and she slipped inside the doors of the local truck stop. As far as a source of information, truck stops were invaluable. Drivers spent hours on the roads and if someone was looking for someone, they were the best place to start for information.

Jessie slipped into the booth, directly behind several truckers she'd seen in the diner. They were discussing their upcoming trips and that slowly changed to discussing the stupid drivers they'd encountered on their latest trip.

"Anyone else see a dark suburban about? I don't normally pay much attention to non-descript vehicles like that, but this one is a long way from home. California plates are kind of hard to miss."

"I saw that vehicle in Rawlins two days ago. I can't imagine what took them two days to get here."

"Someone said they were looking for a girl. Something about her having stolen a lot of money."

Jessie cringed and started shaking. *So that's how he's getting people to cooperate with him. I'm a thief. I wonder how much money he's saying I took?*

Jessie listened as the conversation changed to one of speculation about what kind of girl would steal money from someone who looked like Dino and his buddies did. The truckers had been perceptive enough to realize Dino wasn't a lightweight and his buddies were probably hired muscle, but they'd been completely off-base in their assessment of her character.

Floozie. Gold digger. Slut.

The assassination of her character continued until she wanted to lean over the cubicle and swear to them she was none of those things. She wanted to tell them exactly what kind of human being Dino was, but doing so would put her in even greater danger. The fact that Dino was still chasing her after all these years meant he still hadn't forgiven her for leaving him and taking with her the knowledge that could completely destroy his family's entire business.

Jessie had thought about going to the authorities at one point in time, but fear that she would somehow be endangering Zane by coming out into the open had kept her from doing so. She knew Dino and his father operated outside the law and the only way she could see it was possible to do that was that they had the law on their side. Not knowing how far reaching Dominica Salvatori's power went, she took the safe route. Rylor had also tried to get her to open up to him but she'd refused much for the same reasons.

She slipped from the booth and made her way towards the bathroom. After making use of the facilities, she pulled her heavy coat back on and headed out, making her way to the bus station. That was where Dino would be looking for clues and confirmation that he was still on her trail. She could only hope that six months had dulled the agents' memories and no one would be able to remember her and Zane's arrival in town.

Jessie didn't really consider herself a religious person, but there had been one foster home who had made sure she was exposed to the idea that there was a God up in heaven who loved and cared for her. She didn't have any personal experience with which to prove that idea, and her life had almost been a disproof for the presence of a loving God, but too many people went to church for it to all be a sham.

Rylor had been the next person to introduce her to church once again. She'd only gone a few times with him but she remembered the preacher being so sure that God was loving and longed to help us in our times of trouble, she said a quick prayer, figuring it couldn't hurt anything.

If there was a God and he decided to turn an ear to her plight, she would be very thankful. If he was only a figment of men's imagination in an elaborate attempt by the church to control people and their actions, then she wouldn't be out anything because she really didn't believe anyway. Jessie was at a crossroads in her life. She needed to move forward and longed to make a proper home for Zane and herself, but as long as someone was searching for her she couldn't do that.

God, if you're really there, I could use a little help. This really bad guy is trying to find me, and I can't let him do that. I have a little boy to protect. Okay, guess that's it.

Chapter 3

Thirty minutes later, Cheyenne Bus Station...

The dark suburban was parked outside the front doors of the bus station and Jessie quickly made her way around to the side entrance, and then found a spot where she could watch Dino and his thugs try to get information that might lead them to her location.

They'd been questioning a ticket agent when she'd first arrived and now were perusing a route map. It appeared they'd come up with a dead end on anyone who might have seen her arrive in town six months earlier. That didn't surprise Jessie, as she'd made a point of keeping a low profile whenever she was in a place where surveillance cameras might be in use.

She'd also been extra careful about using her real name and in fact, hadn't even known her Social Security number until arriving in Cheyenne. Rylor had put in a request for her records from California and at the time, Jessie hadn't really been too worried about Dino finding out. She'd never known her Social Security number and didn't think his family's influence reached to the levels of the federal government. Local cops and politicians – most certainly.

"Miss, can I help you find something?" an elderly voice asked from behind her.

Jessie turned her head to see a uniformed agent standing there. "No, I was just resting for a bit before my bus left. Am I in the way?"

"No, no. You just sit there and warm up. It's a cold one today and that wind is supposed to pick up throughout the evening. You

25

might want to check the departures board. There's a high wind advisory out between here and Rawlins and some of the buses have been delayed upwards of twelve hours."

"Really? I'll go do that now then. Will I be able to stay here overnight if my bus is one of those delayed?"

The gentleman shook his head, "I'm afraid not, but the ticket agent should be able to get you a voucher for a free night's hotel lodging across the street."

Jessie gave him a smile and shook his hand, "Thank you. I'll head down there now. You have a good rest of the day."

"You, too, miss. Remember, be safe."

Jessie nodded and headed for the other side of the large foyer, keeping her head tucked and watching Dino and his goons as they headed for their vehicle. She waited until they were out of the building before changing her course and getting to where she could see them getting into the vehicle. Once they were gone, she went back inside and headed for the ticket agent Dino had been speaking to.

"Excuse me," she said to get the girl's attention.

"Yes, how can I assist you?"

"Some friends of mine were by here a few minutes ago. We're looking for a runaway and think she might have taken a bus through here."

The agent nodded and then smiled, "Tall, dark and too good looking?"

"That describes him perfectly. Did you happen to give him any idea of where this girl might have gone next? It's really important that we catch up with her soon."

"Well, he asked about video tapes and such, but we don't store those films onsite here."

Jessie nodded, "I understand. So, you didn't suggest he head in one direction or another?"

"I told him that if I were a young girl trying to stay off the radar, I'd probably head south towards Fort Collins, Colorado. He informed me he'd already been to the bus station there and surveyed the tapes. The girl he's looking for didn't come from Colorado."

Jessie hid her dismay as the girl continued to talk, giving Jessie lots of information she could use. It seemed that the ticket agent had correctly assumed that she'd come from the western part of the state. "So you think he's headed north?"

The agent nodded her head, "I did tell him that. He wanted to know about Laramie but I told him I didn't think there'd be many places to hide there. Too flat."

"So, towards… what's the next big city north of here?"

"Gillette. I'm fairly certain that's where they were headed next. The man did say that they were going to spend the night in town and he gave me his number, just in case anyone else remembered anything."

"You've been lots of help," Jessie told the girl as she backed away from the counter. "Thanks."

Jessie made her way back towards the exit and then headed out into the day that was quickly turning to late afternoon. The sky had turned grey and it looked like the wind had picked up and brought along a nice snowstorm to further aggravate things. *None of these buses are leaving tonight.*

Jessie headed back to her small apartment, not sure what to do next. The only option she really had left was to contact Dino and see if she could assure him she wasn't ever going to tell anyone what she knew. Unless she could get Dino to leave her alone, she and Zane would never be safe.

She ducked into the library and headed for the pay phones located on the basement level. As she waited for the call to connect, she could only hope that Dino hadn't changed his number after all of these years. It began to ring, and Jessie felt her mouth go dry.

"Whoever is calling me better have a damn good reason," came Dino's irritated voice.

Jessie opened her mouth, but nothing came out. She took a calming breath and tried a second time. "Hello, Dino."

Silence greeted her for several long moments and then Dino's sardonic laugh reached her ears. "Well, well. If it isn't the little lost girl. Tired of running yet, baby?"

"Don't call me that. Why are you still trying to find me?"

"Who says I am?" Dino fired back.

"I heard you were looking for me in Wyoming. Desolate place with miles of nothingness but wind and snow this time of year. Not a place I enjoyed very much," Jessie told him, hoping the shakiness she was feeling in her body wasn't coming through in her voice.

"So, you're saying someone in Wyoming tipped you off that I'm there looking for you? It seems you were paying attention and learned a few things from me after all."

"You don't have anything I want to learn. Why are you trying to find me? I have a new life now and I have no intention of ever coming back to California."

"Ouch! Never is a long time, baby."

"I already told you to stop calling me that. If you're worried I'll tell anyone what I know, you should know by now that isn't going to happen. I wouldn't do that to myself. I want to forget everything that happened back then. You have my word…"

"I don't want your word, Jessica. You still don't get it. You are mine. I had such great plans for the both of us… I groomed you, I took you off the streets, fed and clothed you, protected you… and you chose to repay me…"

"Dino, you're trafficking people. Teenage girls. Girls just like me, except they probably have families that love and miss them. I thought I knew you…"

Dino gave another laugh, "You saw what I wanted you to see. I tell you what, you tell me where you are, and I'll come get you. We'll go back to San Francisco and pretend the last six years never happened. You can stick your head in the sand and pretend I'm just a nice businessman. I won't tell you about my work and you won't ask. How would that be?"

Jessie started shaking her head, not caring that Dino couldn't see her actions. "No. I'm never going back. I don't want to have anything to do with you or your lifestyle… I just want to be left alone."

Dino was quiet for a long while and then he spoke again, striking fear through her heart. "Nice try, baby. My guys just returned from searching that little closet you call an apartment. They didn't find you, but surprisingly enough, they did find evidence that you don't live alone. I'm disappointed in you, Jessica. It seems you've been keeping a secret."

"The kid things belong to my roommate. I couldn't afford a place on my own so I sleep on the couch."

"A roommate. I thought you had moved on from Wyoming?"

Jessie realized too late that she'd just given up the fact that she was still in Cheyenne. "The minute I heard you were in town, I did just that. Maria took her kid and she's gone, as well. Go back to California and leave me alone."

"No can do. So, I'll tell you what I'm going to do. If you truly did skip town when you first heard I was here, you have maybe a two or three hour start on me. The last bus that left was headed to Gillette. I'm going to get a goodnight's sleep and then in the morning, I'm going to come and find you. If you're smart, you'll be waiting at the bus station when I get there. If you're dumb, well, my offer to rejoin the family and myself will be retracted. Instead, when I catch you – and I will, you'll be finding yourself in the same category as the women you were so upset over. Another piece of human flesh helping to line my pockets in some South American brothel. Your choice… baby."

Dino disconnected the call and Jessie stared at the receiver as tears streamed down her face. Dino was never going to stop looking for her. She wasn't safe to remain in Cheyenne and she didn't dare take a chance on going to get Zane before she left.

Rylor's words came back to her mind along with the instructions for where she should go if she ever found herself in need of a safe place to stay. She trusted Rylor to do the right thing for Zane and she could only hope that when she didn't show back up to get her son tomorrow, Rylor would take him home to Warm Springs for his sister's wedding. She'd make her way there and retrieve her son and then they'd disappear once again. This time, she wouldn't stop until she got to the other side of the country. She'd change her name and her appearance and hopefully, in time, she'd find a place to finally call her own and where she could raise her son. Zane deserved to have a better life than she'd had and to do that, she had to get them both as far away from Dino as possible. It was the only way to ensure their safety.

Chapter 4

The next day...

If Rylor had been worried when Jessie left Zane with him, it was nothing compared to the worry and actual fear that was stalking him now. Jessie hadn't shown up last night, nor had she arrived this morning to retrieve her son and provide Rylor with the explanations he needed. Zane didn't seem to be minding overly much, but Rylor could feel that something wasn't right.

On his way to pick up dinner last night, he'd swung by Jessie's apartment only to find the door ajar and everything inside destroyed. The meager furniture had been smashed, the food had been tossed from the cabinets and the fridge, to cover the floor of the small kitchenette. Rylor was glad he'd requested Zane stay in the car, but now he was worried about the child's safety. A quick glance around showed him that all of the clothing that had been left behind had been shredded to ribbons, and not even Zane's toys had escaped unharmed. Whomever was after Jessie meant business and had intended to send a very strong message. One that had fear running through Rylor's veins.

He'd continued to hold out hope that Jessie would show up this morning, but it was almost afternoon and Zane was still his responsibility. He gave the quiet little boy a fake smile and secured him in his car seat. Zane had grown quieter as the morning had gone along and his mother had yet to show up. *Jessie, I don't know where you are, but you owe me a huge explanation.*

They arrived at the airport and Rylor held Zane's hand as they waited for Jerricha to deplane. She was getting married to Logan

31

James two days from now and Rylor had no choice but to take Zane with them as they headed back to his childhood home. Warm Springs.

Jerricha's smiling face appeared and Rylor waved to her, releasing Zane's hand as his sister jumped into his arms for a hug.

"Hi!" Jerricha squeezed his neck hard.

"Hi yourself. I'm assuming this greeting means you had a good time in the studio?" Rylor asked. Jerricha had just taken a huge step in her music career by going out on her own as a solo act. She was just returning from having her first recording session on her first solo album.

"It was awesome." She continued to chatter on about how much she'd gotten accomplished and how impressed everyone had been as they retrieved her luggage. The entire time, Zane just watched her silently.

She finally noticed him when Zane reached for Rylor's hand. She looked from Zane to him and asked, "Uhm, Rylor, do you need to tell me something?"

Rylor squeezed Zane's hand in support and made the introductions. "This is Zane and he's going to spend the weekend with me because his mother has to work. Do you mind if he comes to your wedding?"

Rylor knew there was going to all sorts of explanations required, but Jerricha simply gave him a look and then squatted down to greet Zane. "Hi, Zane. So, you're hanging out with my brother? That's pretty neat. Would you like to come to my wedding?"

Rylor was relieved when Zane nodded before sticking his thumb into his mouth. Rylor gently pried it out and swung him up into his arms. Rylor knew the thumb-sucking was a defense mechanism Zane only employed when he was feeling confused and nervous. "Let's get this show on the road."

Rylor felt relieved when Zane fell asleep shortly after they got onto the highway. The winds weren't as bad as the day before, but the snow that had fallen during the night was dry and swirled around the road. Visibility wasn't as bad as it could be, so Rylor counted them lucky on that count.

Zane stopped at Laramie and ordered food for all three of them, waking Zane up so that the little boy could eat before hopefully resuming his nap. Rylor wasn't disappointed and as they got back onto the highway, Zane's eyes slowly drooped and he fell asleep once more.

Jerricha wasted no time in starting her interrogation. "Okay, start talking and do it fast before he wakes up."

Rylor gave her a lopsided grin and explained what he knew. "Zane's mother is missing. He's been in and out of so many foster homes, the state is considering terminating her parental rights and making him available for adoption."

"How old is he?"

"Five. Jessica is trying to get her life together, but her past keeps catching up with her. She dropped Zane off at my office yesterday, saying she needed me to watch him for a few hours while she took care of some things. I've... gotten close to her. Closer than I probably should have, but there's something about her that just catches me right in the gut."

"How old is Jessica?" Jerricha asked, sensing how torn her brother was over this situation.

"Twenty-three. Jerricha, the life she's lived... you can't imagine how much she's been through." *And I only know a small fraction of what she's endured because she won't tell me what I want to know. That ends now, provided she ever comes back home.*

Rylor told Jerricha what he knew and how he'd come to meet Jessie and Zane and how he'd been able to help her get on the road to building a new life for herself and her son. When he got to the part about Jessie asking him to watch Zane, it sounded bad.

"Are the authorities looking for her?"

Rylor shook his head. He told her that he was hoping Jessie was headed to Warm Springs and how he'd told her to seek refuge there if she ever ran into trouble and he couldn't help her.

"Jerricha, I think she's in real trouble."

"Rylor, I think you should call the authorities in on this one. Don't you kind of have to in your position?"

"I'm walking a fine line right now. The only thing saving me is the fact that I've been working with the FBI on a human trafficking case for the last five months. They'll have my back if things start unravelling." He wasn't sure what Jessie was involved in but he was tempted to contact his FBI connection and see if they could answer some questions for him. As much as he loved social work, lately he'd been made aware of the fact that there were very little options for women who found themselves in need of a place to start over.

He'd been toying with the idea of starting a safe house where women who had been rescued from human trafficking or street prostitution could get the help they truly needed. A safe place to both emotionally and physically heal. That was his vision, he just wasn't secure in the knowledge that he was the one to spearhead such an effort.

"So, what are you thinking about doing?" Jerricha asked, her express showing that she understood the heart break of women who found themselves in this position. Jerricha had travelled enough, there was no way she'd been exempt from witnessing the street prostitutes selling their bodies for cash and hoping it was enough to keep their pimps happy so that they could live for yet another day.

One could find them in every area of life in the big cities. Many of them became victims of the sex trade by being kidnapped and forced into it and never found a way out. Others got hooked on drugs and ended up doing anything just to get their next fix. If they ended up getting pregnant, they then had the added burden of dealing with an abortion or worse yet, bringing a child into their sordid living situation.

It was a cycle of degradation no human should ever experience and Rylor found himself in a unique position of being able to do something to help those fortunate enough to be rescued from that lifestyle.

"Rylor, if you get this project off the ground, know you've got my backing. I've been looking for a cause to support. Looks like I just found it."

"Thanks, Jerricha. That means a lot."

"If you can even help one woman it will have been all worth it."

Rylor smiled at Jerricha, "I'm glad you feel that way. Do you remember the old logging camp on the back side of the mountain from the house?"

"I do but didn't it shut down years ago?" Jerricha asked.

"It did, but I've been doing some research and it's for sale. I'm thinking of buying it and turning it into a safe house. I was worried about staffing such a facility but then I remembered the good people of Warm Springs. So many of them have conquered adversity and wouldn't mind sharing their experiences with people if it was seen as useful."

"You seem to have given this a lot of thought."

"I have. I also have investors waiting in the wings to make this happen. I just... I need to get this situation with Jessie figured out first."

"Ry, I's gots to go potty," a small voice called from the back seat.

"Hey, buddy. Hang on just a few minutes. I'll take the next exit."

"I can't wait. I's gots to go right now."

Rylor looked at Jerricha for help, but she shrugged.

"You could pull off to the side of the road," she suggested. "It's already dark outside."

"There are two feet of snow on the sides of the road. There's a turn off up ahead." He put his signal on to switch lanes and then told Zane, "Hang in there buddy. See that green sign up ahead? That's the bathroom. We'll be there real quick."

Rylor got them to the gas station in record time and was out of the car and carrying a very antsy little boy towards the men's restroom before his sister could even offer to help. Rylor wasn't sure how long Zane could hold it and, in his opinion, he'd already been risking the interior of his car by not pulling over the minute Zane had spoken up.

After washing Zane's hands and his own, he swung him up and carried him back to the warmth of the car. He opened the door and then asked Jerricha, "Do you need to use the facilities before we get back on the road? We have another hundred miles or so to go."

"I'm good. Zane, are you feeling better?"

"Yes."

"Good." She waited until he had them back on the highway before she told him about calling home.

"I spoke to Kaedon and kind of gave him a brief rundown of what's been happening. I told him there was a possibility Jessie might be headed to Warm Springs and he's going to let Tom know to keep his eyes out."

Rylor sighed and then gave Jerricha a smile, "Thanks for doing that. Did you also think to have Kaedon warn mom about Zane's arrival?"

Jerricha flashed him a smile, "Of course. I've got your back, Rylor. Just like you've had mine so many times in the past. It's what family does for one another."

Rylor gave her a sad smile and then shook his head. "No, it's what our family does for one another. Many families are that in name alone. Jessie was trying to keep from recreating her childhood, but it seems circumstances keep preventing her from doing that."

"With you on her side, she'll come out okay. You won't settle for anything less."

Rylor gave her a smile of thanks and then turned his attention back to the road and the rapidly falling snow. *God, if Jessie is still out there in this weather, please keep her safe and deliver her to Warm Springs so that she can be reunited with her son. She needs help, I just wish I knew what or whom was threatening her. At least then I'd know what kind of weapon to bring to the fight. Jessie girl, you have some explaining to do. And soon.*

Chapter 5

Sunday, January 13th,

Warm Springs, Wyoming...

Jessie hunkered down behind one of the tall planters in the large reception hall, her eyes darting around nervously as she searched for the only person in the world who meant more to her than her own life. Zane. Her son.

She tried not to think about how she was dressed and instead, focused on the beautiful people milling around the room. She'd gotten a glimpse of the bride in all of her wedding day finery and knew they would probably be very upset if they knew she was there, dressed in torn and dirty jeans and a shirt that had definitely seen better days.

Three days earlier, she'd been forced to leave her son behind as she ran for her life once again. She'd been running for more than six years and had started to believe that maybe she'd finally run far enough away from the streets of San Francisco that she and her son could finally start putting down roots and making a life for themselves. After speaking with Dino, she knew now that was never going to happen until she disappeared for good.

Jessie had done some thinking as she made her way across Wyoming to Warm Springs and she'd come to a few conclusions. First, Dino Salvatori was one of the worst examples of a human being Jessie had ever had the misfortune to meet. She hadn't realized how evil he was when she'd first met him. He'd looked like her knight in shining armor. At the age of fourteen, Jessie wasn't naïve by any stretch of the imagination, but as she became more aware of how Dino made his money, she found herself too scared to get out. At the age of seventeen, she'd discovered just how evil a human being could be and she'd known that if she didn't get out she'd be lucky to see her eighteenth birthday.

Dino had hidden his wickedness for so many years that she hadn't immediately realized how things were changing. The night of her seventeenth birthday Dino had taken her to a fancy restaurant, given her a bracelet with lots of sparkling stones in it, and announced he didn't want to just be her friend any longer. He'd told her how he cared for her and wanted to be her boyfriend. Even now she couldn't think about that time in her life without wanting to throw up.

Jessie's life hadn't been a walk in the park by any means. The first ten years of her life she'd been shuffled from one foster home to another. Most of them only took in foster kids because of the monthly paycheck that came with them. They didn't want to nurture homeless and parentless kids, they simply had found an easy way to make a living. Jessie had grown used to being ignored and neglected but the last foster home she'd been sent to had shown her that there were worse things than being ignored.

There had been almost a dozen foster kids living in the same home and the older boys had decided to start a little side enterprise of their own. At the age of eighteen, they'd been fresh out of school and learning quickly how to work the streets. As pimps. They'd been selling the other foster kids to line their own pockets and the worst part was the foster parents knew what was happening and did nothing to stop it.

Jessie had only been in the home for a week when one of the older boys had invited her to a football game. She remembered feeling special that he'd paid attention to her and she'd been excited about her first date. Only, it wasn't a date to watch the football game, but to hang out beneath the bleachers and let his friends and anyone with a ten-dollar bill take liberties with her juvenile body.

Jessie's life had forever changed that night. At one of her previous foster homes she'd been able to learn some self-defense moves from one of the older girls. She'd put everything she knew into defending her person that night beneath the bleachers and she'd rushed from the stadium, with only a few bruises on her body and her trust in humanity broken. For nearly a year, she avoided the police, the social workers who came looking for her, and the homeless people who wouldn't think twice about getting rid of a young teenage girl.

Then she'd met Dino. It had been raining that night and she'd been drenched to the bone and shivering beneath the stairwell in an alley behind a restaurant in the downtown area. Dino had found her there nearly frozen to death. He'd immediately pulled her out of her hiding place, rushed her inside the back of the restaurant, made sure she had something dry to wear and then fed her.

If she'd known then what she knew now, she would have stabbed him in the heart with the first knife she could have grabbed. Dino Salvatori was a demented man who lived by his own set of rules and got rid of anyone in his way or who thought to try and control his actions. He was a god in his own mind and unfortunately for Jessie, he had decided that she was his. His property. His protégé. His to control and command. He was obsessed with her, that was the only way she could explain why he was still looking for her six years later.

Movement across the crowded room caused her to gasp and cover her mouth with a hand. *Zane.* Her eyes opened wide and a big smile spread across her face. Her little baby was growing up so fast.

Her eyes took in his appearance, his neatly combed hair and the way he was smiling and enjoying himself. He was playing with several other children that looked to be about his age and he didn't appear to have a care in the world. From across the room she could hear his laughter and it warmed her mother's heart. She watched him for several minutes, wishing she could give him this sort of life all of the time.

Was I ever that carefree? Did I ever have a life that brought such a genuine smile to my face?

Jessie started to go to him, but then she remembered how she was dressed and shame forced her to stay hidden. She'd torn her jeans yesterday morning and the scratch beneath had bled a bit into the remaining fabric. Her sweatshirt had been ratty before she ran for her life and was now dirty and stained with a whole variety of things. She raised a hand to her hair and cringed at the feel of the knots there. She was a mess and not fit to move about with the nicely dressed people who were gathered to celebrate someone's wedding. Rylor had said his sister was getting married, the famous singer, and Jessie stayed hidden not wanting to embarrass Rylor. They were friends and true friends didn't hurt one another. Rylor was her only true friend and she couldn't afford to lose him. Leaving him would be hard enough and a part of Jessie hoped they would be able to remain long-distance friends.

She stayed hidden, willing Zane to move in her direction. If she just bided her time maybe he'd come close enough she could get his attention and they could sneak out of the building without anyone being the wiser. She didn't have a plan for where they would go next, but she'd seen several barns on her way into town and she figured she and Zane could hunker down there for a night and then in the morning, she'd figure out a mode of transportation. She'd not seen a lot of semi-truck traffic coming into the town but they had to receive material goods once in a while.

She couldn't stay put now, so if a truck didn't come through tomorrow, she and Zane would just have to make their way to the next town and hope for better luck there. No matter what, she needed to stay on the move. Dino and his thugs were sure to find their way to this small town eventually and she wouldn't be responsible for anyone else getting hurt because of her. She already had to bear the guilt for two lives.

Several months after running away from the women's shelter, she'd been staying at a homeless shelter and two older women had befriended her. Jessie had been confused, experiencing morning sickness at all hours of the day and night, and these two women had taken her under their protection. Two of Dino's thugs had shown up at the shelter and Jessie had panicked. She'd quickly explained that they worked for the man who she was running from and they'd helped sneak her out the back door of the shelter. Dino's thugs had seen them sneaking out and followed them. While Jessie had been running down the alley to get as far away as she could from the men who wanted to hurt her, Mary and Nanette had been stonewalling Dino's men. They'd been beaten up for helping her to escape and their injuries proved fatal the next day.

Jessie was so consumed by guilt, she spent the next six weeks isolated and alone, hiding beneath highway overpasses or sleeping beneath park bushes. Each time she closed her eyes she couldn't help but see the two women who'd sacrificed their lives for hers and her baby. She didn't think she could stand being responsible for anyone else getting hurt or killed. Her heart couldn't bear that, just like it would never survive being back under Dino's control. She'd rather die than allow that to happen.

Maybe I should just leave and let Zane stay with Rylor? At least that way I'd know Zane would have a chance at having a normal life. A life with someone who cared about him and only wanted the best for his future. I could leave Rylor a letter and maybe he'd adopt him.

It didn't matter that Jessie wanted the same things for her son that other mothers wanted, she wasn't in a position to give them to him. She would never be in that position. All she could do was keep running and hope that this time they would outrun the distance Dino was willing to chase her down over.

Jessie watched Zane a few moments longer, smiling as she saw him doing an excellent job of communicating with kids his own age. She was so intent on observing her son, she didn't sense the man creeping up behind her until it was too late, and she'd been ensnared.

Suddenly, a large hand had covered her mouth and nose, making breathing hard. She opened her mouth to scream, but the hand covering her mouth simply tightened its grip. She couldn't even get her teeth into the hand cutting off her sound and making breathing difficult. She arched her back and kicked backwards, but it felt like a giant had taken ahold of her. The arms of steel banded around her, squeezing until she stopped struggling and then lifted her clear off her feet.

The giant didn't toss her over his shoulder, he simply held her plastered against the front of his body as he carried her from the reception room and down a narrow hallway. She kicked her feet, taking a small amount of pleasure when her heels connected with his shins and he grunted in pain, but his response was simply to lift her further off the floor and squeeze tighter.

A door was opened with his foot and then closed the same way. He strode towards a small couch and Jessie could see that she was in a small ante room of some sort. A large crucifix stood at the front of the room and several prayer benches sat before it.

When the giant set her down, she immediately scrambled sideways, climbing over the arm of the couch and placing it firmly between herself and her attacker. Her breathing came in ragged bursts and she could feel herself starting to panic. Her vision was narrowing, and she struggled to control her breathing before she passed out. There was no telling what this stranger would do to her if that were to happen.

Zane.

Her son's smiling face from moments before swam in her mind. She had to deal with this lunatic and then get to Zane. They had to get away before Dino started expanding his search beyond Gillette, something that had probably already occurred since she was supposed to have been waiting for him a few days earlier.

She took one calming breath and then another before meeting the grey eyes of her handsome... *Wait! You can't seriously be thinking about things like that right now. Get it together, Jessie.*

Her little self-lecture over, she forced herself to hold the man's gaze. "Who... who are you?" she asked in a shaky voice, clenching her hands into fists at her sides as she awaited his answer. *Please be a friend and not a foe. I can't handle another enemy right now. I really can't.*

The giant who'd picked her up held out a hand to her in supplication. "My name is Kaedon Ballard. I'm Rylor's older brother." He paused and then added, "You're safe here. I'm sorry if I scared you, but we've been looking for you and I didn't want you to take off before Rylor had a chance to talk to you."

Jessie eyed him carefully. He was easily several inches over six feet tall with broad shoulders and callused hands. He'd carried her and now wasn't even breathing hard. She lifted her eyes back to his own and then asked, "Did Rylor talk to you about me?"

"Not much. Just enough for us to know that you might be in a bit of trouble."

Jessie rolled her eyes and murmured more to herself than to him. "That's an epic understatement."

"Want to tell me about it?" Kaedon asked softly, not willing to ignore her last words.

Jessie shook her head, "Not especially. Want to go get my

little boy and let me get out of here?" Her snarky tone didn't go unnoticed and based on his expression, wasn't appreciated either.

Kaedon gave her a small smile and then asked, "You just arrived. Why the hurry to leave?"

The door opened, saving her from having to answer, and Rylor stepped inside the room with Zane carried in his arms.

"See, I told you Mommy's here," Rylor murmured in the little boy's ear. He set him down on the ground and gave him a little push. "Go see her."

Zane ran across the floor and threw himself into Jessie's arms, tears of joy running down both of their faces. "Mommy! Mommy, I thought you left me forever!"

Jessie hugged Zane close to her chest, her own tears wetting her cheeks. "I'm so glad to see you. Were you having fun? And look how nice you look."

Jessie kissed his little cheeks and then held him close, breathing in his little boy scent. This was her reason for living and she was never going to willingly leave him behind again. Never.

Chapter 6

"I mentioned her being in trouble and she confirmed that fact. Is she likely to bring that trouble here?" Kaedon asked Rylor, keeping an eye on the young woman as she talked with her little boy. They'd moved off to the side of the room a bit, keeping themselves between the mother and son and the exit.

Kaedon couldn't seem to take his eyes off of her. When she smiled, her entire face lit up, and she transformed into a beautiful girl. Her hair was knotted, dirty, and he thought it was probably a golden blonde, but it was hard to tell since it was so dirty. Her clothing looked like she'd been living in it for several days, and based on what Rylor had said, she probably had been.

Her eyes were a dark blue and so expressive, Kaedon could read her like a book. Her voiced reached him across the room and he watched her interacting with her son in a way that screamed of her love for him. She was... Kaedon stopped himself, finding it disconcerting that he was noticing anything about this stranger.

He turned to look at Rylor and saw that his brother was also watching the interaction across the small room. "How old is she?" Kaedon asked.

"Twenty-three. She'll turn twenty-four this year."

Kaedon looked at his brother curiously, sensing there was more than a clinical interest there. "You have a thing for this girl?"

Rylor shook his head. "Not in the way you mean. I've come to care for her, but it's a purely platonic emotion. Why? You're not interested in getting to know her, are you? I mean, Jessie's a great girl, but she's got some problems to work through and well... her life's pretty messy right now."

"And that matters, why?" Kaedon asked, curious as to what point Rylor was trying to make.

"Well, we all know how much you dislike messes of any sort."

Kaedon turned away from Rylor and didn't answer. He just waited and watched. There was something about the young woman that called to his protective instincts, and he knew he'd be more than willing to go to battle for her and her son. He'd had a chance to get to know Zane over the past day and a half, and the little tyke was bright and full of questions once he got to know a person. Before then, he was wary and Kaedon had his suspicions that someone, some adult, had been less than kind to Zane in the recent past. Kaedon hoped he might have a chance to help set that individual straight. It would give him great satisfaction to do so.

Again, Kaedon found himself puzzled over the strange pull her felt for this young woman. Zane had already stolen his heart. The little boy was imaginative, smart, and had a sense of humor that had made Kaedon laugh more than once in the last two days. The little boy was a survivor and no matter how hard life had been, he seemed wired to find the good in it.

Looking at Zane's momma, Kaedon was sure she'd been subjected to her own version of abusive treatment, only for her it had definitely been worse. Just thinking about anyone abusing Jessie had a fire building in his gut. Kaedon had seen a lot in his thirty years on this planet, and nothing got him riled up more than a man who thought he could put his hands on a woman in anger or lust when it wasn't reciprocated.

"She going to be staying here for a while?" Kaedon asked.

Rylor nodded. "More than likely. I got a call this morning and it looks like the safe house idea is moving forward. I have to go back to Cheyenne in a few days to get things started."

Rylor met his brother's eyes and then added, "I'm not sure exactly what's going on, but it's not safe for Jessie there, so yes. I'd like to leave her here, where I know she'll have people watching her back."

Kaedon gave him a brief look and then nodded once. "Consider it done. I'm renovating the school auditorium for the rest of January and February. I'll make sure she stays out of trouble and has a chance to heal from whatever sorrows this life has brought her way. You know the parents will help, as well."

"I appreciate that. But a word of caution, brother. Women who have been through as much as Jessie has often don't have any confidence in their judgment skills. What I mean is she might welcome your friendship today and then tomorrow she'll think about something and she'll have your actions all twisted up and meaning something entirely different. You'll need to take it slow and easy with her. Communication is really important with women coming from her background."

"I'll keep that in mind." Kaedon and Rylor realized that enough time had passed for Logan and Jerricha to have left the reception honoring their wedding and wasted no time in getting Jessie and Zane moving, as well.

Rylor walked over to Jessie and Zane. "Jessie, we're going to get you and Zane someplace safe for the night. Do you have anything else with you?"

Jessie shook her head and Kaedon was sure he saw tears glimmer in her eyes. *She hates being dependent upon people, especially men, to meet her needs. She wants to stand on her own two feet, but life has taken that away from her. I intend to find a way to give her that freedom back. Someway. Somehow.*

Kaedon moved to stand next to her, as well, and lifted Zane

into his arms, "Ready to go, little man?"

Zane grinned and nodded, "Cake?"

Kaedon chuckled and then nodded, "Yeah, we can find you some cake before we leave."

Jessie opened her mouth to respond, as well, but a look from Kaedon had her closing her mouth. He smiled at her self-control. "Jessica, do you like wedding cake?"

She watched him and then swallowed and asked, "Depends on what kind. Any of it chocolate?"

Kaedon nodded, "I imagine so. I can't imagine a wedding reception without a chocolate cake."

Rylor spoke softly to both he and Jessica. "I'm going to go find mom and dad and let them know you're here. Zane has been sleeping in the guest bedroom and there's plenty of room to stay with him there or I can find you a bedroom of your own."

Jessie immediately started shaking her head, "I'll stay with Zane. We're used to sharing."

Kaedon gave a nod and then gestured for her to precede him through the door. Rylor went down the hallway to the right and Kaedon, Jessie, and Zane turned and headed the opposite direction. After securing several pieces of chocolate cake from the reception counter, Kaedon settled at a table towards the back with Jessie and Zane.

He watched as Zane swiped a finger through the frosting and then sucked it off. "Good?"

Zane eagerly nodded, taking another swipe and ignoring the fork his mother held out to him. Kaedon switched his gaze and it locked with Jessie's. "So, Rylor tells me you're in a bit of trouble, possibly from your younger days. Care to elaborate on that?"

Jessie's face closed down, "I was in trouble, but won't be for much longer."

"Why is that?" Kaedon asked.

Jessie took a long time answering and when she did, he knew she already had a plan in mind and it was suddenly very important to Kaedon that she share that plan with him. With Rylor. With the family that was now going to be putting their lives in jeopardy trying to protect her and her son.

Jessie played with her cake and then spoke softly, "I've identified the problem and now know what I have to do to make it go away. I've come to terms with that…"

"Come to terms with what?" Rylor asked, taking a seat next to her and looking between her and Kaedon.

Kaedon sighed and then informed his brother, "It seems that whatever problem sent her running from Cheyenne is still around, but she's now figured out how to deal with it. I was just getting ready to inform Jessica that she will be telling us about this problem, in great detail and let us be the judges as to whether or not she has the problem adequately handled."

Rylor nodded and then met Jessie's troubled gaze, "You did promise to do just that when I agreed to help you with Zane."

Jessie looked like she wanted to bolt and Kaedon hoped she wasn't that silly. Her face was so expressive, and he watched as she explored the various options she had for grabbing Zane and trying to leave without being detained. He also saw the recognition settle in her eyes when she realized she didn't stand a chance. But it was the defeat in her eyes that tore at him.

Unable to sit quietly and watch her spirit disintegrate, he leaned forward and captured her gaze. "Jessica, telling us what danger is threatening you and Zane isn't admitting defeat. Asking for help doesn't make one weak, it shows ones' strength in their ability to realize their limitations. Let us help you. Hasn't Rylor proven he can be trusted? I'd ask the same about myself, but you don't know me well enough to answer that question." *But you will. There's something about you I need to figure out.*

"You two... Rylor, you don't know..."

"So, explain it to us," Rylor told her. "We can't help you if we don't know what's lurking out there."

Jessie shook her head and after several minutes of internal debate she finally gave up. "Fine. I'll tell the entire sordid tale and then you'll see that my solution is the best and only way to ensure Zane and I won't be in danger any longer." She paused and then looked around as if just realizing they were still surrounded by people dressed for a wedding and still enjoying the reception. "Not here..."

"No, this is not the right place. We'll do this back at mom and dad's house. Let me go tell them what's up. I think they should be there, as well as Tom..."

Jessie started and shook her head, "Who's Tom?"

"The law in Warm Springs," Kaedon informed her. "If there's a possibility that trouble might follow you here, he needs to be in the know. Don't worry, he's one of the good guys." Kaedon slid from the table, murmuring that Rylor should take this time to get both Jessie and Zane back to the house up on the mountain. He'd follow as soon as he could and then they'd find out exactly what they were dealing with.

Once they knew what or whom was putting that look of fear in Jessie's eyes, they could then put together a proper plan to take care of it. In Kaedon's mind this situation was just like renovating a house. Sometimes you had to strip everything away, down to the studs, and start building from the ground up. He would shore up any parts of the frame that were weakened and he'd end up with a beautiful product that would last another hundred years.

Jessica was definitely in need of some shoring up and for some reason he couldn't identify, Kaedon was willing to step in and take on the responsibility that came with doing so. The only deterrent he saw was his own brother. It was obvious that Rylor cared for Jessica and her son but Kaedon wasn't convinced it was only platonic. He'd made the mistake of giving his heart away once before and it was still lying in shattered pieces from the experience. He'd have to keep his distance with Jessica – a little voice inside his head warned him that he wouldn't survive another heart break.

His mind turned to the information Tom had shared with him earlier. Marilee was coming home. Back to Warm Springs.

Maybe I'm the one who should be shoring up my own defenses and arming myself against the storm that is sure to arrive with her. She's been gone a long time but the fact that even hearing her name makes my heart ache means she's not been gone long enough for my heart to heal.

As Kaedon drove up the mountain half an hour later, he couldn't stop the feeling that his life was about to get very complicated and messy. Kaedon didn't really do messy, in any area of his life. He like things organized and everything in its place. But, as his mom would say, life is messy. Do your best to clean up the messes as you go and don't sweat the small stuff. The laundry will still be there tomorrow, as will the dishes. Choose your battles and don't let the messes overwhelm you.

It was great advice on the surface but acting on it was a completely different thing altogether. He was thankful his mom and dad had agreed to meet them at the house to hear Jessie's explanation. It might be uncomfortable for her but Kaedon knew that she was going to need all of the help they could offer her if she was going to get through this situation and come out on the other side whole.

The same could be said of the situation with he and Marilee

and he planned to have a discussion with his family before she arrived so that they understood how things needed to be. Marilee was part of his past and he had no intention of allowing anyone to dredge it up and make it a part of his future. The past needed to stay in the past.

Chapter 7

Two hours later…

In true Susan Ballard fashion, no discussion was going to be held on empty stomachs, nor was little Zane going to be included in the conversation to come. No one had been able to argue with her logic, so a quick dinner consisting of sandwiches, chips and apples was thrown together and eaten off paper plates while seated on the couches in the great room.

Dakota Ballard had insisted on stirring up the fire and Susan had helped Jessica put Zane down for the night, before returning to the great room and preparing to bare her soul and her sordid past to a bunch of strangers. She consoled herself that Rylor wasn't a stranger, but someone she considered a friend, and if he was okay with her telling her story to others, she should be, as well. *This is a safe place. Remember that, Jess.*

A new man was seated next to the fire as she walked back into the room and she hesitated in the doorway until Rylor saw her and urged her to come sit down next to him. She glanced around the room and realized the seat next to Rylor on the couch was the only one left. It also left her facing everyone else in the room. *The hot seat.*

"Jessica," Kaedon called her name and she looked at him. "This is Sheriff Tom. Is Zane sleeping?"

She nodded and sat down on the edge of the couch, clenching her fingers together in her lap. Rylor touched her arm and she let out the breath she'd been holding.

"Relax. Everyone is here because they want to help you."

"I know," she began softly. "It's just... I haven't told anyone... I thought that would keep me safe..."

"But?" Rylor asked when she didn't continue.

"He's obsessed and nothing is going to keep me safe unless I completely disappear. First thing in the morning I need to figure out a way to get to the East Coast..."

"Wait up a second. The East Coast? Of the United States?" Rylor asked, his voice going from soft and comforting to one filled with alarm and disbelief. "Jessie, you can't just run away from your problems."

Jessie looked at him and nodded, "It's the only way I can disappear. He keeps finding me because I'm not running far enough away. He's banking on that. If I jump several different states, change my name and my appearance, maybe he won't be able to find me..."

Kaedon held up his hand and stopped everyone else from talking. "You've kind of lost us, Jessica. Let's take a step back and you answer a few questions for us. Let's start with putting a name to the man you keep referring to."

Jessica swallowed and then shook her head, "I can't. It's too dangerous."

Tom leaned forward and assured her, "It's only dangerous if we don't know who we're supposed to be looking for. Give us his name."

Jessica looked at everyone and even Rylor wasn't giving her a way out of answering this question. "His name is Dino Salvatori..."

"What?" Rylor asked, his voice having risen to an almost shout. He glanced at his mom, realized he was now hovering over Jessie, and then apologized, "Sorry, but she just took me by complete surprise."

"Do you know Dino Salvatori?" she asked fearfully.

"Not personally, nor do I want to. His name has come up several times in the last few months in connection with a case I've been working on. How do you know Dino?" Rylor demanded to know.

Jessica told them how Dino had found her and rescued her off the street. The longer she talked, the more comfortable she became until she was talking freely about her life before it all fell apart. She only slowed down when she got to the night of her seventeenth birthday.

"I really thought he liked me and that I was finally going to get the family I'd always wanted. I already had a good case of hero-worship going on and he played me."

"What happened after that? Did you marry him?" Susan asked softly.

Jessie shook her head, "No. That would have made things so much harder. For several weeks things were perfect. He treated me like I was made of glass. I really thought I was in love with him, that I was finally going to be part of a family. And then... well, I wanted to surprise him with a picnic lunch... I made the food all myself and packed it up in this little wicker basket... I went down to the distribution center because he'd told me that was where he was going to be spending the day."

"Had you ever been there before?" Tom asked.

Jessie nodded, "Several times, but only in the front offices. No one was there when I arrived, so I headed into the back of the building - the warehouse portion. It has docks and that makes it easier to unload the freight that comes in from all over the place."

"Did you see something that day?" Rylor asked.

Jessie nodded, "A part of me wishes I hadn't seen it, but then

I'm glad I got my eyes opened..." She took a moment and then looked up, fixing her gaze above everyone's heads. "Dino was supervising a new arrival, but it wasn't furniture or clothing... a woman fell out of the truck."

Jessie paused for a moment as the memory of that young girl toppling to the floor of the warehouse replayed in her mind. She could hear the young woman's cry of pain and fear. Jessie recalled gasping and then covering her mouth with her hand so that she wouldn't give her presence away.

"She was blindfolded and her hands were secured behind her back. She was so young..."

She lowered her gaze and saw that her words had not been what any of them were expecting, except for Rylor. He didn't look surprised at all. "You knew?"

Rylor shook his head, "No, but the Salvatori name has been mentioned more than once in connection with a human trafficking investigation I'm involved in. How many women were there?"

"Eight. All of them teenagers. Dino's thugs were asking them questions and being abusive... I didn't know what to do..."

"Did Dino see you standing there?" Tom asked.

"No, I moved backwards but I couldn't make myself leave. Not yet. I didn't want to believe what I was seeing. The Dino that was in that warehouse wasn't the same man I'd known for three years and... I was in shock."

Susan reached over and clasped her hand, "No one would want to believe another person capable of such depravity. What happened next?"

"They started unloading the rest of the cargo. I'm not positive, but it was a white powder... There were two pallets and each one had these packages about the size of a small suitcase... they were wrapped in paper and plastic."

"You're talking about drugs?" Kaedon asked.

Jessie nodded, "Lots of them. Maybe cocaine?"

"Or heroin. There are rumors that the Salvatori cartel is moving both," Rylor quietly interjected.

"Cartel? No, Dino's Italian, not…."

"The feds think they are closely connected to a very strong cartel in South America…"

Jessie's ears began to ring as Dino's threat came rushing back at her. He'd threatened to send her to a South American brothel… he was so much eviler than she'd thought.

"What were you just thinking?" Kaedon asked her, leaving her no room to not answer.

"Dino said something about South America when I talked to him…"

"You spoke to this monster? When?" Rylor demanded.

"I called him from the library in Cheyenne. I needed to know how he was finding out where I was. I've been only using the buses because they don't get your name when you buy the ticket at the counter. He's been watching security footage and following me from one place to another. I think he would have already caught up to me but he has responsibilities back in San Francisco he can't ignore."

"For six years?" Tom asked. "He must be really worried that you're going to talk to the authorities."

"That's why I called him. To find out. I wanted to assure him I just wanted to be left alone. That I wouldn't talk about anything I'd seen or knew. But I don't think it's fear I'll talk that is driving him. It's me. He wants me back."

"What else did you two discuss?" Tom asked.

"He thinks I went to Gillette and he's probably already fanning out and trying to figure out where I went. He doesn't know about Zane, not really. His thugs tore up my apartment and I convinced him I had a roommate with a little kid. If he ever finds out about Zane…"

"Is Dino Zane's father?" Rylor asked.

"Yes. After finding out what Dino was doing I tried to pack and leave but he came home early. I confronted him with what I'd seen and he locked me in our bedroom." She broke off and swallowed back the bile that rose in her throat. He'd done much more than simply lock her up, making her pay for disappointing him and trying to run in much more physical ways. He'd let Tony rough her up a bit, as well, but most of her abuse had come directly from his hands.

"Did he hurt you?" Kaedon asked softly.

Jessie nodded, refusing to give details about this aspect of her life. She took a breath and then moved ahead with the story. "Three days later, I finally figured out how to get away from him and after he left, I popped the hinges on the door and slipped out the window and down the fire escape. I went to a local women's shelter and I thought I would be safe there. It seems the director of the facility and Dino are good friends. She called him, and he showed up there with one of his goons."

"Let me get this straight," Rylor stood up, pacing now in obvious anger. "You went to a women's shelter and they called your attacker? That's unbelievable, even for California."

Jessie nodded, "The Salvatori family has lots of connections and they give a lot of money to certain causes. I couldn't let him find me. Not after what the nurse had told me."

"You didn't know you were pregnant, did you?" Susan asked kindly, still holding her hand.

"Not until then. It had only been three weeks… Dino had always kept the guys away from me while I was growing up."

"So, Dino didn't know you were pregnant?"

"No and after speaking to him a few days ago, I don't think the nurse said anything, either. She must have not entered it into my chart."

"That's a good thing," Rylor told her. "So, Dino has been following you around using the bus cameras and such. Did he tell you what he wants?"

"He offered to let me come back and we could go back to pretending I hadn't seen anything at the distribution center. He'd do the same and life would go on. He's obsessed with me."

"Sounds like it," Tom said with a nod. "So, he was headed to Gillette? How many days ago was that?"

"Two. I was supposed to be waiting for him there Friday."

"So he's had two days to put out feelers. How did you get here?" Tom asked.

"A series of truck drivers. I hung out at the truck stop on the interstate until I found someone heading this direction."

"Which means you were probably seen by more than one person. It wouldn't take long for someone with access to those tapes to figure out what direction you headed."

"We should assume Dino knows she was headed here and plan accordingly."

Talk ensued about the various ways they were going to monitor the highway coming into town. It was the only way in or out of Warm Springs this time of year and being that the holidays were over, visitors to the town were normally at an all-time low during the month of January.

"Jessie, you look beat. Why don't you come into the kitchen with me and we'll make some hot cocoa?" Susan suggested, rising from the couch and receiving grateful nods from the men in the room.

"Don't I need…"

Kaedon stopped her, "You've done enough. Go with mom and see if you can't convince yourself you're safe here."

Jessie dropped her gaze and nodded once, following Susan back into the kitchen in silence. On one hand she was proud of the way she'd held it together to tell her story, but on the other hand, she felt so exposed and vulnerable right now.

Susan must have picked up on that because Jessie found herself encased in a hug, "It's going to be alright. My boys aren't going to let anything happen to you and they'll figure out a way to get this person out of the picture for good."

"Short of killing him and his family, I don't see how that's going to happen."

"Well, let's table the discussion about killing Dino for later. I'm not saying the man probably doesn't deserve it for the lives he's ruined, but I find I rather like the idea of letting the law do the dirty work. Rylor's been working with the FBI for several months now and I'm sure he'll be sharing with them this new knowledge. Maybe it will be enough for them to put him away for a good long time."

"Maybe." *I'm just tired of running and living in fear. I need this to end, even if it means I have to become someone else. Whatever it takes to keep Zane safe and away from Dino.*

61

Chapter 8

Kaedon looked at his brother, his dad, and his friend. "Anyone got any ideas of where to start?"

"I think you should contact your FBI friends and clue them in on what you've just learned. Maybe the information Jessie can provide is the break they've been waiting for." Their dad, Dakota, didn't believe in beating around the bush and that seemed the most direct route to getting a handle on this situation.

Rylor nodded, "I was thinking the same thing. It's already late, so I'll make the call in the morning. How do we safeguard the town and the people living here? If Dino finds out this is where she's at, who knows what he might do."

'

"I'm going to put two men on round the clock surveillance of the highway coming into town. I'll station them out by the elementary school, which will give us some time to mobilize if the need arises.

"I'm also going to alert the authorities over in Drummond and Rapid Falls."

"Badger Pass is still closed. No one can get here from Rapid Falls," Dakota reminded Tom.

"I'm aware of that, but there are several people with choppers in Rapid Falls. I don't want to be surprised by this guy landing in the middle of town without us having any forewarning."

Everyone nodded and then Kaedon spoke up, "Jessie and Zane need to be with one of us at all times. I don't like the idea of leaving her up here on the mountain alone with mom."

"Agreed," Dakota nodded. "Your mother is more than capable of shooting anyone trespassing on our land, but I'd just as soon not put her in that position. Rylor, how long are you staying?"

"I was planning on a couple of days, but now...I think I need to get back to Cheyenne and put things in motion to keep Jessie safe. I've also got a meeting with the company who owns the abandoned logging camp on the other side of the mountain."

"When's your meeting with them?" Tom asked.

"A phone conference tomorrow but I'm thinking I might move that to an in-person meeting. I have a meeting with my FBI contacts already scheduled."

"When is that meeting?"

"Wednesday. I'll leave tomorrow and plan on coming back here after the meeting. I may bring my FBI contacts with me at that time."

"Good," Tom agreed. "This is their territory and they have many more resources than I have at my disposal."

"Okay, I think we have a plan in place. For now, Jessie and Zane will either be with me up at the high school or with dad when he's staying close to the house."

"I'll get that surveillance set up tonight and we'll wait to hear from Rylor when he gets back. Let's keep her out of the public places, as well. I don't know what's gotten into this town, but it seems like everyone has decided to broadcast the life and times of Warm Springs all over social media." Tom had a disgusted look on his face and the others concurred.

"Maybe someone should talk to Martha and ask her to keep Jessie and Zane's presence here quiet?" Rylor suggested, knowing that the grocery store owner was one of the busiest gossips in town. "I know she saw us leaving the reception hall."

Tom chuckled and shook his head, "Martha's response would be to notify everyone via Facebook that they needed to keep Jessie and Zane's arrival in Warm Springs a secret."

"Does the woman not understand how social media works?" Rylor asked.

Kaedon and Tom shared a laugh and then Dakota spoke up, "I think that's the point Tom is trying to make. Martha doesn't understand how it works and no one wants to be the one to tell her. Just think, if she thought there was a possibility that her thoughts or words could reach people around the world, she'd be a menace to society."

Kaedon had to agree, having known the woman most of his life. "She means well."

"I agree, but that doesn't mean we should lead with the chin. Let's just keep the two of them out of the public arena as much as possible. That should be good enough for now," Tom suggested. "I'm going to head out. You all have a good night and tell Jessie she needs to stop looking like we're all going to hurt her. Nothing gets to me more than seeing that wounded and terrified look in a woman's eyes. It's just not right."

Kaedon walked Tom to the door, "I hear you on that one. We'll do our best to make her feel safe and secure. I'll stop by and see you in a few days, unless you contact me first."

"Will do."

Kaedon shut the door and then resumed his seat just as his mom and Jessie returned to the room with cups of cocoa and cookies for everyone.

"Where did Tom go?" his mom asked as she set the tray down on the coffee table.

"He had some things to take care of. So, Jessica, it looks like

64

you and Zane are going to be hanging out with me for the next few days. I'm renovating the auditorium over at the high school in town. I like to get started early and will want to leave around 8 o'clock in the morning. Is that going to be a problem?"

Jessie looked at him and then at Rylor, "Why do I have to stay with him?"

"I'm heading back to Cheyenne in the morning and no, before you ask, you and Zane can't go with me. I need to know you're someplace safe. If Dino is trying to retrace your steps, he's going to be headed back, or already in, Cheyenne."

"If Dino finds me, not even this town will be safe."

"Then we have to make sure he doesn't find you. The sheriff is posting twenty-four hour surveillance men at the only road leading into town. Dino won't be able to drive into town without us knowing about it beforehand."

"If that's the case, why can't Zane and I just stay up here on the mountain?"

Susan smiled at her and explained, "I would like nothing more, but unless one of the men are going to also be here, I just wouldn't feel safe knowing your protection fell solely to me."

"I'm not helpless," Jessie argued.

"No one said you were, but do you know how to shoot a gun? That's what might have to happen if Dino and his thugs get up here. Could you shoot the man while looking him in the eyes?"

Jessie swallowed and then nodded, a fierce look taking over her face. "If he was threatening Zane, you bet I could. Right between the eyes."

Kaedon and Rylor shared a grin and then Kaedon nodded, "Good. I like your attitude, but none of us are comfortable with putting you or our mom in that position. Therefore, where I go, you and Zane go. For now."

He watched until she finally accepted the way things needed to be and then he smiled at her. "Don't worry about it. I'm sure I can find something for you to do to keep you occupied."

In truth, Kaedon's mind was already making a list of the things that would be safe for her and Zane to help with. He couldn't expect them to just sit idly by all day long and giving them a task to perform would help relieve their boredom and keep her from dwelling on her current situation. He'd always found that giving his hands a task to do gave him clarity and focus in other areas of his life. *Let's see if it works for Jessica, as well.*

Chapter 9

The next day

Fremont County High School...

Jessie looked over to see how Zane was doing with the small task Kaedon had given him and laughed to see her son had invented his own version of how to sort nuts and bolts. Instead of putting them in piles, he had started threading them onto a piece of string he'd found somewhere. She been somewhat hesitant about going to work with Kaedon that morning, not wanting to be in his way and also not sure what she and her rambunctious five-year old were supposed to do all day long. Her fears had been quickly put to rest when they arrived at the school and she'd seen the project Kaedon was working on.

The auditorium was filled with original hand carved railings and trim work, all of which was slated to be taken down and refurbished. It was painstakingly slow work, but Jessie had watched Kaedon strip the years of dirt and grime off of the first piece, revealing the beautiful wood underneath and she'd been sold.

She'd seen the surprise on his face when she'd picked up another piece of wood and mimicked his steps, smiling in joy at her finished product a few minutes later. She looked around the auditorium and then offered, "I can keep doing this if you have something to keep Zane out of trouble for a bit."

"Really?" Kaedon had asked, a dubious look on his face.

"Sure. It's like opening a present because you never know what the original wood is going to look like until you're finished. I can handle this for a while and you can do something else."

"Thank you," Kaedon had told her sincerely. "I don't think I've ever had someone offer to do this type of work for me before. Most people run out of the room screaming at the thought of doing something so tedious."

"That's because they don't have the right attitude."

"Maybe," he'd agreed. "Okay, something for Zane to do... I have just the thing." Kaedon had retrieve a large cardboard box full of nuts and bolts and then showed Zane how to put them into piles. Zane had immediately taken to the task, stating he was going to finish up really fast so that Kaedon could show him how to use the power saw.

Jessie was sure the look of horror on her face at the mere suggestion had been comical, but Kaedon had held it together and suggested that Zane might want to learn how to use a wrench and a screwdriver before he tackled power tools. When Kaedon had glanced at her, she'd seen the mirth in his eyes and she mouthed, "Thank you."

That had been two hours ago, and Jessie couldn't remember the last time she'd felt so relaxed. She wasn't worried about money, Dino, or what was going to happen a few hours from now. She turned to see Kaedon standing on a ladder, carefully removing the molding from around one of the viewing boxes.

Not wanting to startle him and risk him taking a tumble, she waited until his feet were both back on the ground before saying, "You were right."

Kaedon set the wood in his hands down and looked at her, "I usually am, but humor me. About what?"

"Conceited much?" Jessie asked with a teasing smile.

"When I'm right, I'm right."

68

"Wow! Well, I was talking about your statement last night... about keeping one's hands busy kept their mind occupied and didn't allow time to dwell on the negatives. I just wanted you to know you were right."

"Thank you, I'll take that as a compliment." Kaedon looked over at Zane and started laughing, "Son, what kind of sorting is that called?"

Zane had now gone from stringing the bolts together to seeing how many he could stack on top of one another before they fell over. Zane looked up with an impish grin and proudly announced, "Metal blocks."

Jessie chuckled and told Kaedon, "Blocks are his new favorite toy. I'm not sure what he enjoys more, stacking them up, or making explosion sounds when he knocks them over."

Kaedon smiled, "Knocking them over. It's a guy thing."

Jessie gave a snort and then walked over to help her son pick up the mess he had made by knocking his towers over and scattering pieces in all directions.

"It's almost time for lunch. Let's go wash up and we'll head over to the cafeteria. I'd suggest we go by the diner, but that place is second only to Martha's grocery store for greasing the gears of the gossip wheel in this town."

"It's okay, I've kind of gotten used to keeping a low profile. When I first fled San Francisco, I didn't go very far. I took the bus to Sacramento and thought I'd be fine. I didn't realize that Dino's network extended to neighboring cities. I headed north next and ended up in Oregon for a bit, but living on the streets was really hard and not looked at favorably by the citizens and local police. I was pretty sick then, as well."

"Why didn't you seek out another women's shelter?" Kaedon asked as he picked Zane up and they headed for the bathrooms just down the hall.

"I did, but then I overheard them talking about convincing me to give up my baby for adoption. They didn't think I was smart enough or strong enough to handle being a single mother."

"I guess that was two strikes and you didn't go for a third?" he asked. "Hold that answer until we get washed up. Little man, let's go get the dirt off your hands and face."

Jessie went into the ladies' restroom and washed up, taking a look at her reflection and wondering if Kaedon saw the dark circles under her eyes and the way her face was a bit too thin. Jessie had always been blessed with a thin physique, but after taking to the streets, she'd gotten even thinner, bordering on looking ill. Rylor had insisted she see a doctor several months back and she'd been put on a vitamin supplement and told to eat an absurd number of calories each day until she gained some weight. Jessie had taken the vitamins and eaten more, but nothing close to what had been recommended.

The stress of living, paying bills, taking care of Zane, and staying one step ahead of Dino had taken a toll on her body and she knew that wasn't going to change any time soon, so why worry about being a few pounds underweight. Rylor had even quit commenting on it once she'd explained her thinking to him, instead he made sure he always had some decadent calorie-laden treat for her and Zane during their weekly progress sessions. What he didn't know is that Zane usually ate his and most of hers.

She exited the bathroom to see Zane riding on Kaedon's shoulders, a smile a mile wide on his face. "Mommy! Lookee how high up I am."

Chapter 10

Jessie smiled at Zane and squeezed his foot, "I can see that."

Kaedon smiled at her and nodded towards the hallway, "Let's go get some food. The school kids should all be back in their classes by now. I sent a message to the staff this morning letting them know we'd come eat after the kids."

"Doesn't that make them all stay late? I hate to put anyone out…"

"Stop worrying and relax. They always have some food leftover and the staff doesn't eat until after the kids anyway." He swung Zane to the ground and then took his hand.

Jessie reached out and took the other and as they traversed the halls of the school, Zane discovered he could pick his feet up and swing back and forth on the hands of the two adults. Jessie smiled down at him and by tacit agreement, she and Kaedon began to swing their arms while listening to the happy sounds of her son's giggles echo down the hallway.

"Shush, Zane. You're going to disturb the classes," Jessie reminded him when he started to get too loud.

They reached the cafeteria and she was relieved to see three older ladies were just filling their own plates and preparing to sit down. "Kaedon, get in here and eat while it's still warm. Introduce us to your new friends."

"Patty, this is Jessica and her son Zane. They're helping me out with the auditorium renovation for a few days."

"Lovely to meet you both. Zane, would you like some chocolate milk with your lunch?" Patty asked.

71

Zane looked up at Jessie and at her nod, he smiled, "Yes, please."

"Oh, and manners, as well. Son, I may have to have you come back during lunch tomorrow and teach these teenagers a thing or two."

"Now, Patty, you know today's kids are just in a hurry."

"Belle, I don't care if the school is on fire, there's no excuse for poor manners. Jessica, you just keep on teaching little Zane here how to do things correctly."

Jessie nodded and smiled. It was the first time anyone had complimented her on her child-rearing skills and she found it was kind of nice to have her time and efforts recognized. Kaedon moved closer and whispered in her ear, "She's right, you know? You've done a remarkable job with Zane, especially given the circumstances you've been dealing with. Good job."

"Thanks."

Patty set about filling two plates with a large amount of food and then a smaller plate for Zane. The menu for the day included lasagna, salad, green beans, and fresh baked bread with garlic butter. For dessert, there were slices of peach cobbler or chocolate cake.

"Here, dear. You take your little one's plate and Kaedon can bring yours and his."

Jessie took the plate and walked to the nearest table, "Zane, time to eat." She saw her son's eyes go wide at the amount of food on his plate and his loud whisper asking, "Mommy, do I have to eat it all before dessert?" brought smothered chuckles from all of the adults.

"I think you could eat a good portion of it and still save room for dessert. How does that sound?" Jessie asked with a smile.

Zane nodded and climbed up on the chair. He immediately dug into the lasagna and bread, completely ignoring the salad and green beans. Kaedon arrived with their plates and murmured for her ears only, "A kid who thinks like I do. Carbs first, vegetables only if there's room."

Jessie sighed and then dug into her own plate. The food was amazing and she complimented the ladies several times during the meal. When Belle arrived with dessert on a tray, Jessie immediately got up and took the tray from her hands, "Let me do that."

"Oh, thank you. I admit my strength isn't what it used to be."

"Belle's retiring at the end of this school year. She and her husband are going to move to Arizona to be near their grandchildren."

"How many grandchildren do you have?" Jessie asked.

"Ten and one great-grandchild on the way," Belle told her with a smile.

"That's amazing," Jessie commented. "I'm sure your family is going to love having you living so close. Especially if you cook for them."

"Oh, my kids cook just as well as I do," Belle informed her. "How about you dear? Do you like to cook?"

Jessie wasn't sure how to answer that and Belle changed her question, "Do you cook?"

Jessie shook her head, "Not very well. I've taught myself a few things by watching those cooking channels on television, but I never had anyone show me how to cook."

"Your mom didn't cook?" Patty asked.

"Uhm... I was in the foster system while I was growing up..."

Kaedon came to her rescue then. "Ladies, Jessie really isn't comfortable talking about her past. Why don't we give it a rest for now?"

They all nodded and then Belle brightened, "Why don't you stop by the kitchen tomorrow and I'll show you how we make bread. Zane can even come and help."

"Oh, but Kaedon…"

"…will survive one morning without your help," he informed her. "She'll be here, ladies. Now, we need to get back to work. Jessie, eat your dessert, the day's wasting away."

The ladies took their cue and started clearing things away. Jessie watched for a moment and then asked, "Do you think it's a good idea for me to spend time with them? Won't they tell people?"

"Maybe, but I think it's okay. Just remember that you don't have to answer their questions and it won't be rude to tell them to mind their own business. They'd probably congratulate you for putting them in their place if they crossed a line you weren't comfortable with."

Jessie nodded and then reached over and wiped Zane's mouth. He had evidently enjoyed lunch and even now his eyelids were starting to droop. "Somebody's almost ready for an N A P."

"I have a sleeping bag in my truck. I'll grab it and he can settle in the back of the auditorium."

Jessie nodded, once again reminded that she'd allowed her problem to become someone else's. Kaedon had enough on his plate without having to babysit her and Zane, and yet, that's exactly what he was doing. Without complaining.

She picked Zane up, insisting that she was fine carrying him, and followed Kaedon back to his worksite. She sat with Zane for a few minutes after settling him on the sleeping bag, making sure he was sound asleep. She took a few moments to observe Kaedon as he got back to work.

The man was extremely handsome and the more time she spent with him, the more she found herself being attracted to him as a person and not just his looks. She knew he was quite a few years older than her but that didn't seem to matter. He was funny and very organized, patient and encouraging – qualities Jessie had come to look for in people she associated with. Rylor had some of the same qualities, but not once had Rylor's touch on her arm or back ever ignited little sparks up and down her spine. Jessie looked at Rylor like a big brother, and she was confident that was how he saw her, as well.

They'd spent quite a bit of time together over the last several months and he'd become her confidant and sounding board. She knew part of that came from him being her caseworker, but Rylor had never made her feel like his attention was only due to his job. He truly seemed to care about what happened to her and wanted the best for her future.

She got a similar feeling about Kaedon, only there was an undertone of physical attraction with him. She'd never once wondered what it would be like to kiss Rylor, but she'd found herself wondering exactly that several times this morning about Kaedon.

Don't go down that road, Jess. You don't have the luxury of getting involved romantically with anyone. That wouldn't be fair to them or to you. Rylor thinks he's going to fix this, but he doesn't know Dino. The man is a menace and not going to just let this go. You're going to always be looking over your shoulder. Always.

"What has that frown on your face?" Kaedon asked, squatting down so that they were almost eye to eye.

Jess shrugged her shoulders, "Just thinking."

Kaedon shook his head and then grabbed her hand and pulled her to her feet, "Idle hands. It'll get you every time. I have a new project for you, if you're interested. The seats in the upper boxes are just like standard upholstered chairs. The fabric is worthless, but the wood is really grimy and needs cleaned."

He led her over to where one of the chairs stood and Jessie examined the intricate carvings on the arms and legs. "These are beautiful, or they probably were at one time."

"They can be again, they just need some loving attention. Are you up for the challenge?"

Jessie nodded and then pointed to the deep crevasses that were black with years of grime and dust. "How do I clean areas like that?"

Kaedon nodded and then handed her a small tool box. "There are all sorts of things inside there that can be used, but I prefer Q-tips. There are some pointed ones in there that work especially well for getting into tight spots. There's also a bottle of oil soap that will help lift the dirt away from the wood."

"Great. I'll give it a shot." Jessie took the tool box and settled on the ground, the chair in front of her. She immediately went to work on the smooth sections of wood, stroking the dark red grains of wood as they were revealed. "These are going to be gorgeous."

She looked up to see if Kaedon had heard her comment and he was just standing there staring at her. "What?"

"I was just watching you work. Don't ever play poker because you'll be sure to lose every bet. Your face shows everything you're thinking in vivid detail."

Jessie blushed and ducked her head. "I'll remember that," she murmured.

"Don't think too hard about it. There are almost a dozen chairs just like that. I'll bring them all down, but that doesn't mean I expect you to get them all cleaned. They need re-upholstered but there won't be anywhere in Warm Springs that carries the kind of fabric we need. I'll do some internet research tonight and get it ordered."

Jessie nodded and then they both got back to work. She was no longer thinking about negative things, instead she was focused on getting to the true beauty of the chairs, stained upholstery and all. The chairs were kind of like her life, in a away. The years had tarnished and marred their original beauty and they would have remained that way if she and Kaedon hadn't insisted on cleaning them.

My life is tarnished by my past and I don't want it to remain that way. I wish someone could some along and wipe the grime away and just let me shine. That would be nothing short of miraculous.

Chapter 11

Wednesday morning…

Rylor was nervous and he didn't know why. Since arriving back in Cheyenne Monday afternoon, he'd spent most of his time researching the Salvatori family and in particular, the youngest son – Dino. The guy was a hothead and there were rumors about his illegal activity all over the place, but so far, no one had been able to pin any major crime on him. Or the Salvatori family.

Rylor had spoken with his FBI contacts and they'd agreed to fly into Cheyenne to meet with him and to discuss both the situation with Jessie and the possibility of him starting up a safe house for victims of trafficking. They'd been talking to him about the safe house idea for several months and Rylor hadn't realized how close to home the situation was going to get. Now, more than ever, he was dedicated to doing more to help these women recover and heal.

"Trevor, thanks for coming out at such short notice."

"No problem. I understand you might have some information for us and a possible informant on the Salvatori cartel?"

Rylor nodded and gestured for the two men to take a seat. "Brian, how's your wife doing?"

"She and the baby are doing fine. She's not thrilled that I'm still doing field work, but this is who I am and she knew that when she married me."

Rylor smiled, "Glad to hear she's doing well. So, first things first… I have a young woman, twenty-three with a five-year old son, who grew up in San Francisco. Foster system dropout and she took to the streets at thirteen. Dino Salvatori took it upon himself to rescue her."

"What?" Trevor ad Brian exchanged looks. "If you'd told me he pulled her off the streets and started pimping her out, I'd believe you. You say he rescued her? Explain, if you can."

"The best I can figure is Dino knew from the beginning that he was going to try to make her his wife."

"She was what, thirteen? Fourteen? The sick bastard," Brian said with disgust written all over his face.

"I agree, and she was fourteen when she met him. Anyway, he treated her like a princess for three years, until she turned seventeen. Then he took her to a fancy restaurant and told her he thought she was old enough to take their relationship to the next level. She figured they were eventually going to get married.

"Three weeks later, she goes to surprise him for lunch and she's the one getting the surprise. She watched him and his goons unload a shipment of eight women, all blindfolded, crying and with their hands secured behind their backs. She also saw them unload several pallets of drugs – a white powder. She's not sure if it was heroin or cocaine and that doesn't really matter. She estimated the size of the brick and by my count each pallet had over fifty bricks stacked on it. That puts the low-end street value of whatever it was at fifty-million."

"Or more. If it was uncut heroin, they could turn it and quadruple the quantity that actually hit the streets."

"She tried to run and he caught her. She confronted him with the evidence and he didn't deny any of it. She's been running ever since."

"How long?" Trevor asked.

"He's been chasing her down using video footage from bus

stations for almost six years now."

"What else does she have on him? It makes no sense that he would continue to hunt her down if she doesn't have any physical proof."

"The man is obsessed with her. He told her he owns her and she can either fall in line and they can go back to pretending she doesn't know what he does during the day, or he'd find her and she'd join some of the women she felt so passionately about in a South American brothel."

"He actually said that to her? When?"

"A few days ago on the telephone."

"Where is he now?"

"We don't know. He wanted her to meet him at the Gillette bus station on Friday. She's thinking he's probably canvassing all of the surrounding towns and the circle just keeps getting bigger."

Rylor paused and then added, "There's one more piece of information you all should know. Her son, Zane, is Dino's biological kid. And," Rylor held up his hand as both agents opened their mouths to speak. "Before you ask, Dino did not know she was pregnant when she ran from him and it would appear that he's still in the dark."

"Where is she now?" Trevor asked.

"Some place safe and that's all I'm going to say right now. Jessie's not had a lot of chances to build trust in other people and I won't jeopardize the trust she's placed in me. Her location remains a secret for now."

"So, would she be willing to testify against him?"

"I don't know the answer to that question. She has to think about her son and the impact her actions will have on him. I did some checking and she didn't list a father on Zane's birth certificate. I know Jessie hasn't thought this far ahead, but if Dominic Salvatori learns that he has a biological grandchild out there, he'll move heaven and earth to find him and he won't care who he tramples in the process. I would prefer if the identity of Zane's father never leaves this room."

"She's positive Dino is the father?" Trevor asked.

"Yeah. She's absolutely positive. Dino protected her from anything that even bordered on the illegal or immoral while she was with him. I don't how much longer that would have lasted, given his propensity towards depravity, but he treated Jessie like she was made of fine china. His guys weren't even allowed to curse around her."

"This is Dino Salvatori we're talking about, right?" Trevor asked. "The man is as vile as they come. I'm sure he holds some strange sex appeal with his Italian good looks and flashy cars, but the man is a sociopath in the making. People like that don't usually success in playing the upstanding citizen for long periods of time."

"Well, there's something about Jessie that got to him. He wants her back and has spent six years trying to make that happen."

Trevor and Brian conferred privately for a moment and then Brian nodded. "Do you think Jessie would sit and talk with us? Her testimony is great but we're going to need hard evidence before we can seek a search warrant or make any arrests."

"I understand, and she'll meet with you and answer any questions she can. I'll have her in Drummond at the diner there tomorrow at noon."

"Is Drummond where she is now?"

"No. I'm not giving up her location. Not just yet. Now, about the safe house. I've located an abandoned property with dormitories to fit two dozen or more women and children. It will need a lot of work, but it's isolated and there's only one road in and one road out of the closest town."

"Sounds perfect." Trevor pulled a stack of papers from his briefcase and slid them across the table. "The department is willing to underwrite sixty percent of the costs for overhead and that offer indicates they are willing to provide up to $2.5 million in initial investment costs. The facility will be listed as a private entity but will be used exclusively to house and rehabilitate victims of human trafficking.

"That packet lists the various services which you will need to provide. Underage minors will need to have access to private tutors until such time as they can return to their families or begin online schooling. Those who are over the age of eighteen will need to be provided the opportunity to finish their high school work and earn their GED.

"Access to proper medical treatment, psychological counseling, job training and life skills education are also included. We're talking about an entire facility dedicated to helping these women deal with what happened to them, figure out how to deal with the emotional and physical scars they'll never get rid of, and move out into society and function in a normal capacity."

"That's been my goal all along, but this isn't a quick fix. Some of these women may need to be at the facility for years. Some may never be able to re-enter the society they were taken from."

"We realize that and there are other places women who are that damaged can go."

Rylor flipped through the paperwork for a long moment and then nodded his head, "I'll have to read these more thoroughly, but on first glance and hearing you explain what's included in them, I don't see any problems.

"I met with the owners of the property yesterday and they are willing to sell the property to me at a substantially reduced price of $2.8 million. There are over fifteen hundred acres included plus a dozen or more buildings. Some of the buildings will need to be torn down, but those remaining can most likely be renovated and refurbished. I've already got a contractor in mind to oversee this project."

"Really? You've thought that far ahead?" Trevor questioned.

Rylor smiled, "My older brother has a private construction firm. He's got one project on his plate for early spring and then he should be able to start on the safe house compound."

"Well, it looks like we're moving in the right direction on this front. As far as Jessie goes, we really would like to speak to her in person. We'll be at the Drummond diner tomorrow at noon."

Rylor saw the men out and then quickly packed up his belongings and prepared to head back home. Today had gone very well and the feds had offered him more than he'd ever dreamed. With their initial investment, he would not only be able to purchase the abandoned logging camp immediately, but he'd have enough funds to refurbish it and possibly be ready to open by the time summer arrived.

He jumped on the highway and headed home, calling Kaedon on the way to share with him the good news.

"Rylor, where are you?" Kaedon asked.

"I'm on my way back to Warm Springs. Everything okay there?"

"Yeah. Things went really good. The feds want to talk to Jessie tomorrow. I set up a meeting in Drummond for noon. Any chance you could watch Zane while we're gone?"

"Not a problem. That young man is very resourceful. In fact, with Jessie's help, I'm almost a week ahead of my schedule for the auditorium. I'll plan on taking the day off and Zane and I can hang out at the house with mom."

"I'm sure she'd appreciate that. Well, I have all sorts of news to share about the safe house, but I'd rather tell everyone at once. Are Jerricha and Logan back yet?"

"I saw Logan earlier so I'm assuming that's a yes. Want me to have mom invite them up for dinner?"

"Yeah, that would probably be best. If mom's not up to cooking for everyone, call Maggie and see what she can whip up for us and then let me know. I'll pick it up on my way up the mountain."

"Will do. If you don't hear from me assume everything's handled on this end."

Rylor disconnected the call and turned on the radio, not stopping until he found an uplifting Christian station. It had been a while since Rylor had been a regular attendee at Sunday morning church service, but it hadn't escaped him that the adventure he was about to embark upon was going to require more strength and wisdom than he had. He was smart enough to recognize that he was going to need guidance from the man upstairs if he had any hopes of being able to truly help anyone heal.

As the miles passed by, he listened to the music and turned his thoughts towards a name. It needed to be something significant that would bring hope and healing. He tossed many ideas around and then a song came on the radio talking about the freedom to be found when one gives their life over to a loving God. Fear disappeared. Bonds were broken. It was if the song was written just for this time and this moment for Rylor to hear.

Freedom. That's what these women were going to be given an opportunity to grab hold of. Freedom Ranch. He said it in his head and then tossed it around inside the car. He liked the way it sounded and as he headed up the mountain an hour later, he decided to reserve judgment until he could observe his family's reaction. That would be the true test in his opinion.

Chapter 12

Kaedon hung up the phone and then turned, squinting at the silhouette of a person in the rear of the auditorium. "Who's there?"

The figure started walking towards him and Kaedon impatiently waited for them to come into the light and to reveal their identity. When Marilee stepped forward, Kaedon thought his heart might stop. "Marilee."

"Hey, Kaedon. Tom told me this was where I could find you."

"When'd you get back?"

"Yesterday evening. How have you been?"

Kaedon shrugged his shoulders, "Good. You?"

Marilee nodded instead of answering. She walked closer to him and he could tell that not all was right in Marilee's world. Dark circles bagged beneath her eyes, her dark hair was limp and lifeless and haphazardly pulled up into a ponytail atop her head, and her nails were chipped and in desperate need of a manicurist's attention.

"I've been better. Tom told you I was moving back home, didn't he?"

"He did. Was he not supposed to?"

Marilee shrugged and then grimaced, "I guess it really doesn't matter. I'll only be here for a few months, maybe less."

"I thought you were moving home for good. That's what Tom made it sound like."

"Tom doesn't know everything. Well, I mean, now he does, but he didn't before last night. Anyway, I just wanted to come by and say hello. Maybe we could get together some time and talk."

"Marilee, you've been gone more than ten years. I don't see that we have anything to talk about."

"I'd like to talk about what happened... between us..."

"So talk. I'm right here listening," Kaedon told her, unwilling to give her what she was after.

Marilee took another step closer, out of the shadows, and Kaedon could see she'd lost considerable amounts of weight from her last photo shoot just a few months earlier. "Okay, if that's how you want to do this. I owe you an apology."

Apology? "For what?"

"For being selfish and only putting the needs of myself out there. At eighteen, I had stars in my eyes and I didn't care if getting to California inconvenienced anyone or not. It was pretty arrogant of me to expect you and my parents to drop everything and just cater to my whim of the moment."

Kaedon was taken aback and gave her a curious look. "When did these feelings of remorse show up?"

"A few months ago, I had to really sit down and look at my life. The entire thing. Not just the acting or the magazine shoots, but the actual day to day living. I realized that I had been making my decisions based upon what I wanted to happen next for so long, I'd forgotten that sometimes I needed to live in the here and now."

Kaedon watched her for a moment, sensing there was something he was missing. "What brought about this life-altering change in your thinking?"

Marilee took a deep breath and then look directly at him. "What I'm about to tell you, not even Tom knows, so I would appreciate it if you would give me a couple of days to tell him before you say anything."

Kaedon's alarm bells were pinging loudly. He nodded and

then gestured for her to take a seat, "You look like you're about ready to pass out."

"I get tired really easily. That's actually what started all of this. I collapsed during a film shoot about a month ago. They called the medical team and did some basic blood work. They diagnosed me with anemia and a bacterial infection, prescribed some over-the-counter iron pills and antibiotics. I felt a little better after taking the pills and didn't really think much about anything.

"A few days after that, I was scheduled to do another shoot and the photographer noticed I had some bruising on the backs of my thighs. They were right around where the edge of a chair would push into your legs when you were sitting, but they were deep purple and almost black in color. They didn't hurt and I hadn't known they were even there.

"That prompted the medical team to send me over to the clinic for a complete medical work up. It turns out, the bruising was only starting to occur. If I bump into a door or counter top, I bruise. They take days to heal and while they don't hurt, they look pretty awful."

She pulled back her sweatshirt sleeve and Kaedon barely contained the gasp of shock at the deep bruises on her arms. "These were from bumping into things while I was packing my apartment up."

"Marilee, that's not normal. Did the doctors figure out what's going on with you?"

Marilee nodded and then looked away from him. "They did. I have a rare form of blood cancer."

"What?" Kaedon asked, stunned by this news. "What are they doing about it? Radiation? Chemo?"

Marilee shook her head, "There's nothing they can do, at least, there's nothing they can do here in the States. I have a rare form of leukemia that is considered to be incurable. The doctors have said there is nothing they can do, and this type of cancer is pretty aggressive. I already have secondary tumors in my liver, spleen, and lymph nodes."

Kaedon felt like crying and screaming all at once. He looked at the woman he'd once given his entire heart to and couldn't believe what she'd just told him. Marilee reached out and grabbed his hand, "I know this is a lot to take in, but I'm okay with it now. I've made peace with myself and I came home to make peace with you and Tom."

"We need to get you a second opinion…"

"I've already had third and fourth opinions. There's nothing they can do except make me comfortable as the cancer progresses and spreads. That's why I came now. The doctors are giving me maybe until the end of summer, but probably not that long. I don't want anyone to see me when things get really bad. I want everyone to remember me when I'm still somewhat healthy. Like this."

Kaedon shook his head, "Tom's never going to go for that and neither am I. I don't care how bad you think it's going to get, you need to have people who care about you around…"

Marilee gave him a sad smile, "I was hoping you'd understand and help Tom do the same. I've already made the arrangements and I'm not going to change my mind. There's a clinic over in Switzerland that has accepted me. I'm flying there at the end of February. I'll live a normal life until I can't and then they'll see that I have everything I need until the end finally comes. I've instructed them to keep Tom updated when I get too weak to do so myself."

She paused, "I know this is a lot to digest, but life is precious and this is how I choose to end mine. I've had the paperwork drawn up so that when the cancer spreads to my brain and I lose the ability to communicate and function, they will administer a lethal dose of drugs and I will simply go to sleep and not wake up again."

"Marilee are you listening to yourself. You're talking about assisted suicide. Killing yourself."

"No, I'm talking about stopping weeks, maybe months of needless pain and suffering I have no desire to endure. Kaedon, if there was any chance of fighting this illness, I would do so, but all of the doctors agree – the type of leukemia I have is incurable. No one has ever survived it. I am dying."

Kaedon looked at her for a long moment and then stood up, pulling her into his arms and holding her tightly for quite a long time. That was how Jessie discovered them.

Kaedon heard her enter the auditorium and he slowly released Marilee, hoping he didn't look as devastated as he felt right at that moment.

"Should I come back?"

Marilee turned and shook her head, "No, please don't leave on my account. I'm an old friend of Kaedon's and I'm in town for a bit and wanted to say hello."

Jessie nodded and hesitantly walked towards them, "I'm Jessica."

"It's very nice to meet you," Marilee told her warmly. "Are you the mother to the adorable little boy I saw out in the foyer?"

Jessie looked alarmed, "In the foyer?"

Kaedon nodded, "A couple of girls from the study hall class came by and asked if they could take Zane outside to play with a ball they swiped from the gym. I didn't see the harm in it. Was I wrong?"

Jessie shook her head, "No, I'm just not used to him being out of my sight for very long. I'm going to go check on him. Nice to meet you."

Kaedon watched her leave and called after her, "I'm ready to call it a day. I'll be right out."

Marilee was watching him carefully and once Jessie was out of the auditorium, she challenged him, "You like her."

"What makes you say that?"

"The way you watched her. There was a time, long, long ago, when you used to look at me the same way."

"If you're implying I love Jessie, you are way off base. I've only known her since Sunday."

"Who said there's a time limit on how long it takes to fall in love with someone? The heart knows what it wants."

"I'm not in love with Jessie. She's only twenty-three for goodness sake."

"And age makes no difference once you leave high school. I should know, I've been married three times to men twice my age."

"You've been married three times? Why did Tom never mention anything about that?"

"Because I didn't tell him. I barely spoke to him once a year. Besides, all three of my husbands died within two years of us getting married. I decided after number three I was destined to remain single."

Marilee had just thrown him for another loop and he backed up a step, needing some space to absorb everything he learned this afternoon.

"I need to head back to the house. Promise me you won't say a word to Tom until I have a chance to talk to him?"

"I said I wouldn't, but I can't tell you that I'll support your decision to end your life alone and without any family or friends nearby. That's not something I'll ever be able to do."

Marilee nodded, "I can live with that for now. I hope before I leave you'll change your mind, but regardless if you don't, I'm not changing my plans. I'll see myself out."

Kaedon watched her walk out of the auditorium and then he picked up the closest tool and threw it with all of his might towards the stage. It bounced off the wooden frame and landed with a lonely sound on the carpeted floor. He took an extra minute to calm down and then he grabbed his backpack and headed for the exit.

Not tell Tom? How was he supposed to keep a secret of this magnitude away from someone he considered his friend? How was he supposed to deal with everything Marilee had just dropped on him? Nothing he thought he knew about her was true or right anymore. It was like he'd never known her and yet, she was still the same old Marilee. Making decisions about her life and not caring how they affected those around her. In the twelve years since she'd dusted the dirt of Warm Springs off her shoes, she'd not changed all that much. She was still very much all about Marilee.

Chapter 13

Later that evening...

"Rylor, tell us how your meeting went with the owner of the logging camp," Susan requested after everyone had filled their plates and started to eat.

"It went very well. They have fifteen hundred acres and there are over a dozen buildings already standing. Some of them would need to be torn down and rebuilt, but many of them just need to be refurbished and cleaned up."

"Did you discuss a price?" Kaedon asked.

"$2.8 million."

Dakota nodded, "Well, that's a lot of money but not when you consider how many acres of land go with it. Do you have enough investors in this project to cover that big of an expense?"

Rylor smiled, "I won't have to. The feds are going to dish out $2.5 million right off the bat."

"What? But… that's amazing," Jerricha told him with a high-five. "Way to go, baby brother."

"Hold up there with the baby brother stuff. You were only born six minutes before me," Rylor complained, drawing chuckles from the remaining adults.

"Six minutes before you. I rest my case," Jerricha told him with a smirk.

Jessie watched the exchange between the two people, loving how they could tease and argue one with the other and still love one another at the end of the day. She glanced towards Kaedon and could tell he was still upset by what had happened in the school auditorium.

She kept her voice low and asked, "Are you okay?"

She thought she'd whispered the words, but Logan had ears like a hawk, "Why wouldn't Kaedon be okay?" Everyone's eyes turned towards him and Jessie felt like crawling beneath the table. "Did something happen up at the school today?"

"I'm sorry," Jessie mumbled for his ears only. She dropped her gaze to her plate, feeling horrible for having added to his distress.

"Jessie. Look at me," Kaedon's soft voice left no room for not complying. She lifted her head and met his eyes, "You don't have to be sorry for being concerned about me." Then in a normal tone said, "Yes, something happened at the school today. No, I don't want to discuss it right now. I'll let you know if that changes. What I would like to know is what else happened with the feds today?"

Rylor pointed at Jessie, "You have an appointment to speak with Trevor and Brian tomorrow at noon in Drummond."

"Drummond? Why there?" Jerricha asked.

"Drummond is thirty miles from here and just about every place else in Wyoming. I would rather the feds not know where we live and where the safe house is going to be at this point."

"Don't you trust them," Susan asked.

"I trust the men I'm dealing with, but there have been too many mistakes in past raids where the criminals barely got away and were never prosecuted. I think they have a mole in their unit and I'm not taking any chances."

"Good idea," Kaedon nodded. "So, aside from the meeting, what did they say about the safe house?"

"You're not going to believe the offer they made me." Rylor shared with everyone the conditions and requirements that needed to be included in the final facility and Jessie couldn't help but be impressed with the thoroughness.

"I also settled on a name for the place. Freedom Ranch."

Everyone was quiet for a moment and then started nodding. "That's what you'll be giving them."

"Perfect name, son."

"Freedom Ranch... I feel a song coming on," Jerricha murmured, speeding up the eating of her dinner.

When Logan caught Jessie staring at her, he chuckled and explained, "Jerricha gets these song ideas in her head and just has to get them down on paper or track. There have been days where she wouldn't have eaten at all if I hadn't brought the food to her and placed the fork in her hand. At those times, she operates on auto-pilot."

"I guess that's a good thing?" Jessie questioned.

"If you've heard her music, you know the answer to that one," Rylor told her with a grin. "Anyway, I spoke to the owner of the camp and they are having paperwork drawn up right now. I don't have the keys yet, but the owner is having them sent. I'd like to drive over and inspect the property and I was hoping you could tag along and give me an estimate on some of the repair costs," he told Kaedon.

"I can do that. Just let me know when you get the keys and you want to go..."

"I will. I might have to go back to Cheyenne before the keys arrive, but we'll just play it by ear."

They finished dinner in relative silence and everyone simply smiled when Jerricha announced she was finished and darted from the table. "Some things never change," Susan murmured quietly.

Jessie finished supper, encouraging Zane to do likewise and

then she excused herself to carry a very sleepy little boy up to bed. She was gone for more than an hour, and when she returned, only Kaedon remained at the table. The dishes had all been cleared up, and yet, Kaedon was still sitting in the same place as when she'd first gone upstairs.

"What's wrong and don't tell me it's nothing," Jessie told him, sitting down at the table next to him. "Who is Marilee?"

"Marilee is Tom's sister. At one point in time, everyone thought we were going to get married and life happily ever after. I was fully on board with that notion, but Marilee had stars in her eyes and couldn't wait to get out of Warm Springs. Right after graduation, she set up some auditions with a few California talent agencies. She was gone a week and when she came back, she'd scored a couple of commercials and a guest spot on a soap opera.

"She was so excited and couldn't understand why I wasn't happy, as well. She thought I should just pack up and move to California with her. She thought wrong. We argued and the next morning, she was out of here. She hasn't been back since that day."

"Why come back now?"

Kaedon closed his eyes and willed the emotions aside. "I... you can't say anything to anyone about this. She hasn't told her brother yet."

Jessie nodded, "Of course I won't say anything, but this doesn't sound good."

"It's not. Marilee has a rare form of blood cancer that is completely incurable and she's dying."

"Oh no!" Jessie reached over and covered Kaedon's hands with her own, "I'm so sorry."

"Yeah, but it gets even better. This cancer is very aggressive, and people usually suffer for weeks of unbearable pain before they die. Marilee doesn't want to suffer, and she doesn't want anyone here to see her in that condition. She's going to Switzerland and has arranged for her own death when things get really bad."

"She's going to let them kill her?"

"That about sums it up. She told me first because she knows Tom is going to go crazy over this and won't back her. She was hoping I could use my influence to help convince him this was for the best."

"You can't do that, though, can you? You don't think her dying alone and at the hand of another person is the best."

"No. I don't. I told her that, but she's committed to doing things her way. Just like she was when we were eighteen. She doesn't care how her decisions are going to affect others."

"She probably thinks that's exactly why she's making this decision. So that you guys won't have to watch her grow weak and disease ridden. She probably thinks she's saving you."

"Shouldn't that be our decision to make?" Kaedon asked.

"Maybe after she speaks with her brother you can all sit down and discuss this again. She seemed like a reasonable person."

Kaedon leaned his head back and then nodded, "I'd have to agree with that statement. Maybe you're right. She's going to be here until the end of February. Lots of things can happen in that amount of time."

Chapter 14

Thursday, January 17ᵗʰ

Drummond, Wyoming...

"You're sure these agents are the good guys?" Jessie asked as Rylor guided her to a vacant table near the back of the diner. Trevor and Brian had yet to arrive but he was okay with that as Jessie needed a moment or two to calm down.

"Breathe and relax. They aren't going to do anything except ask you some questions."

"I'm trying," she told him.

Rylor reached over and squeezed her hand, "You're going to be fine. There they are now." He stood up and shook both men's hands and then introduced her, "Jessica, this is Trevor and Brian with the FBI. Have a seat."

"Jessica, I'll get right to the point," Trevor took the lead. "Rylor tells me you have some firsthand knowledge about the illegal activities Dino Salvatori is involved in."

Jessie nodded, "I saw him receiving a shipment of... teenage girls and drugs." Jessie glanced towards the large windows, looking for signs that Dino and his men were close. "I don't know if this is a good idea..."

Trevor smiled at her, "Then let me set your mind at ease. After speaking with Rylor yesterday, we put out an APB on the dark suburban with California plates. We also alerted the airports in Gillette, Cheyenne and Laramie. We got a hit early this morning.

Dino was seen passing through security in the Cheyenne airport at 6 o'clock this morning, headed for San Francisco.

"I was curious as to why he would leave when this is the closest he's been to finding you and so I called a contact in California. Dominic Salvatori had a heart attack early this morning and passed away a couple of hours ago. Dino made it just in time to tell his father goodbye."

"Dino went back to California?" Jessie murmured quietly. "What about the goons with him?"

"They are still in Cheyenne, holed up in a motel. We're guessing Dino intends to come back and finish the job of finding you as soon as he buries his father. That gives us a limited window in which to act. His goons – nice title by the way, are here and he's left himself virtually unprotected. With his father dead, Dino is a prime target for the rival gangs. Things were already tense before Dino arrived and now they are turning deadly."

Brian nodded and then asked, "Jessica, can you tell us what you know of the Salvatori businesses. We're particularly interested in the location of his warehouses and distribution centers."

"I've only been to one of them, the one down by the wharf? I know he talked about several more in the shipping district and then there was one somewhere up north. I'm sorry, but I don't remember where."

"That's fine, we'll cross reference the properties owned by Salvatori Enterprises and their various front companies and hopefully we'll get lucky. Now, one last thing for you to consider. Did you ever meet any of Dino's associates?"

Jessie nodded, "A few of them. He always introduced them as business partners."

"Would you recognize any of them?" Brian asked, pulling a stack of photos from his briefcase. He handed them to her and Jessie slowly thumbed through them, selecting more than dozen as being men or women she'd see with Dino or his father.

"That's all of them," she pushed the photos back across the table. "I've seen those people with Dino, but that was years ago. Rylor told you I haven't seen Dino for six years, right?"

"He said you spoke to him a few days ago," Trevor fired back.

Jessie nodded, "I was hoping to convince him to leave me alone. I now know that's never going to happen."

Trevor smiled at her, "I think we can help with that. The San Francisco office has been trying to tie the Salvatori's to human trafficking for years. They've never been able to get into any of their distribution centers because they couldn't get a legal search warrant for probable cause. You just provided that, so thank you."

Brian stood up and shook Rylor's hand and then her own, "Let this guy keep you safe until this is all over. With any luck, Dino will be behind bars before the end of the week and his enterprise will be in shambles."

Neither Rylor nor Jessie were hungry, so they ordered some drinks to go and headed back to Warm Springs. They arrived home and then Rylor stopped her from getting out of the vehicle right away.

Jessie sat silently waiting for Rylor to state what was on his mind. Finally, he looked at her and asked, "Well, what do you think?"

"About what? My name will show up on the court papers granting them a search warrant and Dino's three goons are still in Wyoming. I don't feel safe or happy or anything but scared."

"Jessie, I need you to just be patient and let these guys do their jobs. Now, tell me about Kaedon. How was spending the days with him?"

Jessie blinked at him and then asked, "I guess it was okay. Actually, Kaedon went out of his way to make it enjoyable. I refinished the hand carved wood trim and some of the chairs. He kept Zane busy with nuts and bolts, screwdrivers and wrenches. And I made some new friends in the cafeteria. They've been teaching me to cook."

Rylor raised his brow, "Like, from scratch cooking?"

"The real deal. I know how to make lunchroom bread, honey butter, lasagna, and chocolate cake. But, there's a small problem because all of the recipes I've been making feed two hundred people."

Rylor laughed, "They can be minimized, just do it proportionally and the recipe will still work right."

Jessie nodded, "Proportionally… yeah, I don't know if I can do that. Maybe your mom could help?"

"I'm sure she'd love to. Kaedon could help you, as well. The man is a genius when it comes to numbers, but don't ask Jerricha. Unless something's changed, cooking really not her thing."

"Well, it's not like she needs to know how to cook."

"Everyone needs to know how to cook. It's one of the things I want the girls who come to Freedom Ranch to learn. And how to sew, plant and harvest a garden, make a menu and grocery shop, laundry…"

"…all of the things one needs to have a home and a family."

"Exactly. I want Freedom Ranch to be a place where dreams are reborn, and lives are more than the memories of what transpired in the past."

Jessie leaned towards him, kissed his cheek and then hugged him, "That's beautiful. You should have that made into a motto or something that hangs over the front doors. Maybe Jerricha could even use those words in the song she's writing for you?"

"Maybe." Rylor hugged her back and Jessie allowed herself to relax in his arms for a moment. There wasn't anything in her that was responding to Rylor in a romantic nature, just a platonic sharing of human touch. Something she'd had far too little of in her life.

A tapping on the window brought her head up to see Kaedon scowling at them from outside.

"Uh oh," Rylor murmured. "I've seen that look before. Why don't you head on inside while Kaedon and I have a quick chat?"

"Is Kaedon upset about something?" Jessie asked, confusion on her face.

Rylor shook his head and pushed her back into her own seat. "Everything'll be fine. We'll both be inside soon."

Jessie slipped from the vehicle, puzzled by the fact that Kaedon didn't even look at her, but was staring daggers at his brother. Something was not right.

Chapter 15

Kaedon slipped into the vehicle and shut the door in a very deliberate and controlled manner. Rylor had told him there was nothing between him and Jessica and Kaedon had believed him. After spending the last several days with her and her son, he'd realized the initial feelings she'd evoked within him weren't just a fluke. They were real and needed to be explored.

The instant surge of jealousy he'd just experienced upon seeing her in Rylor's arms was not only disconcerting, but an unwelcome emotion. He was angry at Rylor for leading him astray and at himself for allowing his guard to drop where Jessie was concerned.

"Explain what I just saw, because from where I was standing, you and Jessie were getting mighty cozy," Kaedon told his brother in a soft, controlled tone.

"Kaedon, I know how it probably looked, but there is absolutely nothing between Jessie and I except platonic admiration. We were talking about Freedom Ranch and my dreams for it. Things got pretty serious and intense and she was congratulating me. Like a sister."

"She's not your sister, nor is she mine," Kaedon reminded him.

"I know that but Jessie and I… well, we've had a bond since the very first moment we met. I know she thinks of me like a brother. Ask her."

Kaedon opened his mouth to reply but his phone went off and after glancing at the screen, he shook his head. "I have to go. Zane is inside with mom. Tell her I'll call if I'm not going to be home for dinner. I might be gone a while."

"What's going on?" Rylor asked.

"Nothing I can talk about right now."

"Kaedon, I heard her voice. That was Marilee, wasn't it?"

Kaedon nodded and opened the vehicle's door, "Yes and I'd appreciate it if you didn't ask any more questions. I can't answer them right now because I gave my word." Seeing the questions on Rylor's face, he softened his tone, "Tell Jessica I'm sorry for my behavior earlier and that I hope she'll make some time to talk with me when I get back."

"I'll tell her. Before you go, just answer me one question. Are you and Marilee getting back together? I'm asking because I don't want to see you get hurt again and I definitely don't want to see Jessie get hurt."

"No, Marilee and I are not getting back together and I hope I can tell you what's going on when I get back. It's not good. Not good at all." His phone rang again and he glanced at it before answering it with a terse, "I'm on my way. Give me ten minutes."

He disconnected the phone and then slid from Rylor's vehicle, going to his own truck and heading down the mountain immediately. Kaedon knew he was creating a bad scenario at home, but Marilee needed his help with Tom.

He drove straight to Tom's house and got out, watching as Marilee slowly made her way down from the porch. "I'm really glad you're here."

Kaedon nodded and then looked at the house, "Did you tell Tom all of it?'

"Yes. When I told him about Switzerland, he freaked out."

"What did you expect, Marilee? You tell a man you're going

to kill yourself and that you're dying from a rare type of cancer all at the same time. It's a lot to take in."

"Will you talk to him? Please?"

Kaedon sighed and then asked, "Where is he?"

"In the barn. He wouldn't even talk to me when he left the house."

"I'll go talk to him."

"Hold on a second," she told him, stepping back into the house and returning with a leather coat. "Here, this is his favorite coat, or at least… it used to be."

Kaedon took the jacket and then headed for the barn. He slipped inside and was instantly thankful that Tom had installed a heater for the livestock that wintered there. Kaedon had even helped him install it.

"Hey, Tom. Where are you?" Kaedon called out.

"Marilee call you?" Tom asked from the loft.

Kaedon looked up and nodded, "Yeah, she did. Mind if I come up for a bit?"

"Suit yourself."

Kaedon did exactly that and soon was sitting next to his longtime friend. "Talk to me."

Tom looked at him for a moment and then gave a derisive toss of his head. "Did she talk to you? Did she tell you why she came home after all of these years?"

Kaedon sighed and then settled back against a hay bale. "Yeah, I'm still trying to process it all and she told me yesterday."

"She told you first?" Tom asked, hurt in his voice. "I guess I should be glad she told me at all…"

"Don't be like that. She had some crazy notion that I would be able to help you accept the lunacy she's convinced herself is the right path to take."

Tom turned sorrow-filled eyes towards him, "She's going to let some nameless stranger kill her!"

"Yeah, I got that part. I told her what I thought about that idea and, I hate to say this in light of what's looming ahead of her, but she hasn't changed much. She's still making decisions based solely upon what she thinks is best for her and her opinion of what's best for everyone else. I told her she was wrong, and it didn't make any difference from what I could see."

"Kaedon, she's dying. While that absolutely sucks, what's worse is that she wants to die all alone. I mean, what am I supposed to do with that? Kiss her goodbye at the end of February and forget I ever had a sister?"

"That's not what she's asking you to do," Kaedon told him.

"Sure it is. She wants us to remember her the way she was, so why even come home now? Why not just have those strangers over in Switzerland send us a postcard when she finally kicks the bucket and we could have remembered her the way she was at eighteen? Why even come home now?"

"She's trying to set her wrongs right."

"She's doing a poor job of it."

Kaedon nodded and silence settled over the barn. How long they sat there, neither could have said, but they were there long enough that Marilee finally came looking for them. The barn doors opened and she stepped inside and Kaedon watched as she paused to allow her eyes to adjust to the lighting.

She stepped further inside, pulling the doors shut behind her, "Tom? Kaedon?"

"Up here," Tom identified their location.

Marilee looked up at them, glanced at the ladder and then shook her head, "Can you come down here? I don't think I should be climbing a ladder…"

Tom sat up straight then and asked, "Why? Are you feeling sick?"

Marilee gave a short laugh, "I always feel sick these days. No, my strength and coordination kind of comes and goes… I'd hate to get up there and not be able to get back down. You know what, I shouldn't have come out here. I'll go back inside the house."

Before Kaedon or Tom could call her back, she turned and fled the barn, letting the doors slam shut behind her. "Well, that went well."

Tom looked at him, "Her strength and coordination come and go?" He swallowed audibly and then murmured, "This is really happening. Isn't it?"

Kaedon nodded, "I'm afraid so. I think the question you need to answer now is whether or not you're going to sit quietly by while she decides how this is going to go, or you go in there and tell her how it's going to be, and you don't take any arguments from her."

"I can't make her stay if she wants to leave," Tom reminded him.

"No. That's true. Maybe she just needs to see that leaving would hurt us all more than if she stayed and let us take care of her."

Tom thought about that for a moment and then nodded, "Maybe. I'm going to head back inside. You coming?"

Kaedon shook his head, "No. Marilee and I had our time and it ended twelve years ago. I'll be here to support you both, but this is something you have to work out with her. Alone."

"Yeah. I get it. Thanks for coming over. Tell Rylor when he

gets back…"

"They'd just arrived when Marilee called me. I don't know what they found out, but whatever it is, we'll deal with it. Tonight, your sister needs you. Family comes first."

Tom slapped him on the shoulder and then shimmied down the ladder. He turned just before leaving the barn and looked at Kaedon, "You're a good friend. Thanks."

"No problem," Kaedon called down from the loft. He waited for another ten minutes before he too shimmied down the ladder and headed back up the mountain. He had his own problems to deal with tonight; namely, convincing his heart and his head that Jessie was off-limits. He made a mental list of all the reasons any involvement between himself and Jessie was a bad idea. By the time he walked into his parents' house, he was convinced that any feelings he'd begun to have for Jessie were simply a figment of his imagination combined with too many hours spent in her company.

One look at her face when she saw him tossed all of his carefully constructed ideas out the window.

Chapter 16

Jessie and Zane were stacking up blocks and then knocking them down when Kaedon walked through the door. She'd been concerned at his behavior when she'd seen him last and one look at his face told her there was still something amiss.

"Hi," she offered, watching as Zane hurried across the floor and grabbed his hand, pulling him forward and not relenting until Kaedon had settled on the floor and was dutifully stacking up the blocks.

Jessie swallowed and struggled for something to say. Rylor's only response when she'd asked about Kaedon was that Marilee had called and he'd gone running. Susan had told her how Kaedon and Marilee had been headed for the altar right after high school and how badly things had ended. From what Jessie had learned about Kaedon, he would have had a hard time getting over being dumped for a chance at a career in the spotlight. The fact that she hadn't come home until now was bothering everyone. Something had sent Marilee seeking refuge in her childhood town, but no one seemed to know what.

"How is Marilee?" she asked quietly, hoping to spark a conversation that might provide some answers to the many questions moving through her mind.

"Rylor told you that's where I went?"

Jessie nodded. "He also told me you two were once really close. Did she... I mean, are you two getting back together? Is that why she came home?"

Kaedon looked at her and then answered her question with

one of his own. "What do you feel for Rylor?"

"What?" Jessie was thoroughly confused.

"What do you feel for Rylor? Are you in love with him?" Kaedon pressed her.

"I care very much for Rylor, but not in the way you're implying. Rylor is like an older brother to me. He's helped me with so many things, but I've never wanted to kiss him, not like..."

"Not like?" Kaedon asked, lowering his voice and taking a step towards her.

Jessie swallowed, "Not like... you?" She looked up, realizing that she'd just revealed herself and had no idea of how to take it back. "I...," she broke off, glancing up to see Kaedon watching her intently. She cleared her throat and started again, "Rylor and I are just friends and we help one another. I mean, the relationship isn't equally balanced, but we're just friends."

"I told you that," Rylor said from the doorway leading to the kitchen.

Kaedon looked between them and then shoved his hands through his hair, "I guess I owe you both an apology. I saw you hugging and I thought... well, obviously what I thought was wrong." He reached for Jessica's hand and held it for a moment. "Forgive me for feeling jealous."

Jessie gave him a hesitant smile, "That's okay. I kind of thought the same thing about you and Marilee yesterday." A blush crawled up her face.

Rylor glanced between them and then shook his head, "You two are pitiful." Looking at Kaedon, he added, "You never answered her question about Marilee. And yes, I was eavesdropping."

Kaedon shook his head and then got to his feet, "Where is mother?"

"Here," Susan called, coming to stand beside Rylor. "Zane, would you like to come help me make some cookies?"

Zane knocked the stacks of blocks over with loud sound effects and then hurried towards the kitchen, "Bye, mommy."

Jessie shook her head and began gathering up the scattered blocks. Kaedon and Rylor both did their part and a few minutes later they were all seated on the couches, the blocks safely tucked away in the box they originally came from.

"So, about Marilee," Kaedon began. "She came home to try and right the wrongs she left behind twelve years ago."

"Why now?" Rylor asked. "Those are the types of actions people take at the end of their... lives..."

Kaedon merely nodded in silent agreement with Rylor's sudden insight. "Marilee has a rare blood cancer that is incurable and fast acting. The doctors don't give her longer than the summer."

Jessie looked between the two men, seeing hurt and sadness reflected in both. "She came home to apologize for the way she left."

"Yes, she did. And to let Tom and I know about a decision she has made that will affect all of us."

"Decision?" Rylor questioned.

Kaedon nodded. "She's chosen to go with assisted suicide when the time is right."

Rylor shook his head, "She can't. It's illegal in the United States."

"Which is why she's leaving for Switzerland at the end of February. She came home to say goodbye."

Jessie didn't know Marilee, but the two men sitting near her did and she could see how saddened they were by the decision she'd made without even consulting them. "Did she say why she made that decision?"

Kaedon nodded. "She wants us to remember her as she is now, not sick and weak and writhing in pain."

Jessie nodded, "When I was ten, I was placed in a foster home with an older couple. I was their only foster child and I had my own room… it was one of the best homes I'd been in and I started to think maybe I'd be able to stay there until I graduated from high school. The Jensen's were really kind and devout Christians. They took me to church with them every Sunday and we prayed before every meal. Then Mrs. Jensen got sick. She kept giving one excuse after another to not go to the doctor. When her husband finally convinced her to go, they found out she had Stage 4 Metastatic Breast Cancer.

"They gave her all of the options for radiation, surgery and chemotherapy, but after only a month of treatment, she quit. She said the treatment was making her sicker and she wanted to enjoy the time she had left. She lost weight and eventually couldn't get out of bed without help. It was summer, so I was home all of the time. She seemed to be constantly taking pain killers and I remember thinking at the time that it was so unfair. She was dying but instead of being able to do so with dignity, she was reduced to this being who existed from one dose of morphine to another. She suffered for more than three months before the cancer finally took her life. Three months where she didn't really live and neither did those around her."

Rylor reached out and clasped her hand, "I'm surprised they left you in the Jensen's home during this time."

"They didn't. They removed me the week after she told them she had cancer. My caseworker didn't have a choice, but she did make sure I got to spend several days a week at the Jensen house. They wouldn't let me visit her the last few weeks. The cancer had gone to her brain and she was having seizures. She died and they had a funeral for her. I remember looking at the picture of her they placed on top of her casket. She looked healthy and full of life and so unlike the woman I'd seen the last time I was visited her. No matter how I

111

try, I still can't get the image of her weak, sick body out of my mind.

"If seeing her like that affected me so profoundly, what must it be like for her husband and her kids?"

Kaedon looked at her and then asked, "So you think she's making the wise choice?"

"No one can answer that but her. And Tom. And you. You all have to come to terms with what's going to happen in the coming weeks and months. You might not be able to make that decision now, but in a few weeks... your opinion will change."

"I think what Jessie is trying to say is that we shouldn't worry about next month, or even next week. We should take each day as it comes and make the best decisions we can with the knowledge we have at that moment."

Jessie nodded, glad that Rylor got what she was trying to say. She heard Zane giggling in the kitchen and got up to go see what was going on in there. "My advice, not that it's worth much, is to be glad she's home and do what you can to heal whatever hurts were caused when she left."

She was almost to the kitchen when Kaedon called out after her, "You're pretty good at giving advice, but can you take your own?"

Jessie turned around and knew Kaedon was referring to her belief that the only way to get rid of Dino and the threat he represented was for her to run as far away from him as she could get. Now that the FBI were looking into him, and he'd taken over his father's role in the family business, Dino should have a lot less time to come chasing after her. Still, she wouldn't be truly safe until he and his goons were behind bars.

She gave Kaedon a nod, "I'm trying."

Chapter 17

Several weeks later,

San Francisco, California...

Dino slammed his fist onto the desk and lowered his voice, his anger making him shake. "Find. Her. I don't care what it takes, she's got to be there someplace."

"Boss, she's not in Cheyenne. We've literally combed the town and no one has seen her."

"I wouldn't assume she would still be there. We know she didn't take a bus to Gillette, and she's not visible on the cameras leaving Cheyenne. That means she left by other means. Find her."

Dino slammed the phone down and paced across his late father's office, now his own. He had attacks from all directions and he needed to make sure all loose ends were tied up. Jessica Niles was a loose end that could create significant damage for him. A word to the wrong individual and Dino could find himself the target of a federal investigation.

His cellphone rang, and he answered it with a terse, "Talk." He listened for a minute and then put the phone back into his pocket. He headed for the elevator and after a brief conversation with one of his newest sidekicks, he was headed across town to the distribution warehouse.

He stalked into the warehouse, nodding at the men standing guard at the back of the trailer to open it up. Inside were a dozen girls that had been captured from all over the western half of the United States. Dino stepped into the trailer, looking each girl over and then moving on. When he was finished, he exited the truck.

"Get them out of there and get them cleaned up. Suarez will be here in two hours."

"Boss, is he bringing the merchandise with him?"

"He'd better be," Dino stated with a low growl. He slipped into the office portion of the building and headed for the upper most office. He spent a few minutes taking care of some paperwork and then he headed for the balcony that overlooked the warehouse portion of the compound. He watched as the latest shipment was unloaded and then led towards a holding area. This group of young girls was how he was going to solidify his new role as the leader of the Salvatori family.

Since his father's untimely death, there had been nothing but one challenge after another to his authority. For over ten years, the Salvatori family had enjoyed the peace that came from their enemies knowing how any attempt to change the status quo would be met. Now, it seemed every little faction was attempting to exert their own ideas. That ended tonight.

Raul Suarez had never come to the States to meet his father and Dino didn't want to know what this untimely visit was really about. Raul's demand for a meeting hadn't left any room for negotiation. *I don't know what he wants but I'm ready for him if he's thinking of cutting ties with this family. If I have to make an example of him, I'll do so. Gladly.*

"Hey, Boss," a voice called to him from the floor of the warehouse. "The trucks just passed the first security check point."

"Good. I'll be down shortly. Bring up the rest of the merchandise and make sure all of our boys are in their places."

The Suarez cartel had been supplying a variety of drugs and manual laborers from south of the border and in exchange, the Salvatori family had been supplying their brothels with fresh merchandise, weapons, and a widespread distribution chain for the drugs. It was a very symbiotic relationship and one that Dino wished to continue.

Dino pulled a cigarette from his pocket and lit it before he headed down the stairs. He turned a deaf ear to the sounds of whimpering and crying coming from the pen where the girls had been locked away. The trucks were just coming around the bend in the road and Dino glanced to his right and left and was pleased to see that all of the workers had made themselves visible but as non-threatening as possible. He intended to show Raul Suarez a show of strength.

The trucks slowly backed up to the docks and Dino wasn't surprised to see two armed men disembark from each truck to supervise along with his own rifle carrying men. Raul Suarez also disembarked from a vehicle that had accompanied the trucks and was escorted by two armed men up the stairs. He stopped a few feet away from Dino and nodded his head.

"Welcome. An uneventful journey?" Dino inquired, observing the niceties.

"There was a little trouble at the border but nothing my men couldn't handle. My condolences on your father's passing. I trust you are having no problems?"

"Nothing my men and I can't handle." Dino nodded to his second in command and the order was given to open the trailers and remove the pallets contained inside. Dino walked through the pallets and verified the merchandise was as described and then he nodded to the man guarding the women.

"Bring them," he barked. The women were led from their cage, their hands secured behind them, and a rope used to link them all together. "I think you'll be happy with this lot."

Raul inspected the women, forcing their heads up and speaking in rapid fire Spanish to the man who followed him. Once he was done walking around the women, he gave the order and his men came forward and began herding them towards one of the trucks. The women's cries of distress and pleas to be released increased and Dino turned his back and walked a short distance away to conclude his business with Raul.

"I trust everything is to your satisfaction?" Dino inquired softly.

Raul inclined his head, "And you as well. Our business here is finished. I'll not make this journey again." Raul turned and headed back to the vehicle. The backs of the trucks were closed and the Suarez men all climbed back into them and they began to depart.

Dino didn't stick around to watch the pallets of drugs being dispersed. The men his father had employed knew very well how to handle things on this end. He motioned for his second in command to join him.

"You can handle things from here. Meet any resistance with a show of equal force. I have something to take care of outside of California, but you can always contact me if there are problems."

"Sure thing, Boss. Anything I can help you with?"

"No, just a little hunting expedition. Sam, Jimmy and Tony are already there overseeing things. That's where I was when… Anyway, I hope to only be gone a few more days. You're in charge of things here until I get back."

"Got it. I hope you finally find what you're looking for."

Dino nodded and headed off to where his driver was standing by to take him to the airport. He was taking a commercial flight into Cheyenne, not something he often did, but in this instance, speed was of greater importance than how he traveled.

He arrived in Cheyenne three hours later and strode across the tarmac to see the three men who had been his sidekicks since their high school days lounging inside the terminal. When they saw him, they immediately stood at attention and nodded their heads to him.

"Boss, welcome back."

Dino nodded and preceded them from the terminal and to the waiting suburban. Once they were all in the vehicle, he demanded answers. "Has anyone gone back to the girl's apartment?"

"No one has been in or out of there except the guy who lives in the upstairs corner unit. We're thinking he's either a weirdo or the landlord."

Dino nodded and then motioned for them to begin moving. "Let's go check it out."

The suburban pulled up in front of the small apartment complex a few minutes later. "There's the guy," Tony pointed to a weasley-looking man just coming from the ransacked apartment. "Want me to bring him here?"

Dino nodded and watched as both Tony and Jimmy approached the man and then brought him to the vehicle. They opened the passenger door and Dino invited him to join him. "Please, I just wish to ask you a few questions."

The man climbed inside, his body odor acrid and stinging to Dino's nostrils. "Leave the door open, by all means. Tell me who lives in the apartment you were just leaving."

"No one now. I mean, there was a hot babe living there but since someone tore the place up, I haven't seen hide nor hair of her. I've seen police, that social services dude who likes to check up on her, and two guys in black suits were by here yesterday, but she's just vanished."

"Tell me her name," Dino demanded, cataloging the information the man was feeding him.

"Jessie Niles. The least she could have done was take her stuff with her, now I have to pay to have it removed before I can rent it out again. And she hadn't paid me this month's rent yet. Stupid broad."

Dino reached into his suit jacket and pulled out his wallet, removing several hundred-dollar bills. He held it out to the man, but then pulled it back when the man reached for it. "I'm happy to compensate you for your time and information. I'm very interested in locating the young lady who lived here. I would like you to call me immediately if she should show back up. Can you do that?"

"For that kind of money, you bet I can. I'm Jason, by the way."

Dino chose not to shake the man's hand, instead, he handed him a card with his personal cell phone number on it. "Call me the minute she shows back up. Now, tell me about this social services dude. You say he comes around a lot?"

"Yeah. He's always playing with the kid…"

"The roommate's kid?" Dino questioned.

"If you say so. I don't think Jessie had another roommate, but then again, she didn't tell me anything."

Dino looked at the man and then asked, "Tell me about the kid."

"Zane is his name and he wasn't in school yet. She worked a few odd jobs here and there and was going to school… she took the kid everywhere with her."

"Jason, you have been very helpful. You can go now."

Jason looked at him and then at Tony who now was indicating he should exit the vehicle. "You're sure I can't tell you anything else?"

"Positive. You've been more than helpful. Call if Jessica shows back up."

Dino was seething inside, "Take me to the hotel and then we need to find that slut. She lied to me about the kid and now she's going to pay."

"Whose kid do you think it is?" Sam asked.

"It matters not. She won't be worried about the kid once I find her. I may deliver her to Raul's newest establishment in Colombia myself. But first, we need to find her."

Dino's phone rang and he listened to it only for a few minutes before he started cursing and slammed his hand against the car window. "Get us back to California."

"Boss, what's happened?" Tony asked.

"Suarez didn't leave the country like we originally thought. He was seen meeting with the Koreans and there are rumors that they are joining forces."

"That's insane. If Raul gets caught inside the States, they're going to lock him up forever."

"It seems he's more of an opportunist than I gave him credit for. We're driving straight through, so figure out whose taking which shift."

"What about Jessie?" Sam asked. "And the kid?"

Dino laughed, "Don't you worry about Jessie. She'll make a mistake and give herself away. She hasn't been able to hide from us for six years, a few more days won't matter."

"Boss, this thing with Suarez could take more than a few weeks."

"Whatever. Jessie will be mine, at least for a few days while I make her pay for making me hunt her down."

"And then?" Tony asked.

Dino shook his head, "And then she'll join one of the brothels in the jungles of South America and she'll no longer be a problem."

Chapter 18

Two days later…

The entire Ballard clan, including Jessie and Zane, had made the trek around the mountain to take a look at the logging camp. The weather had been cooperative for the last forty-eight hours, with clear skies and lots of sunshine to help clear off some of the snow. Dakota and Susan Ballard led the way with the snowplow blade attached to the front of the ranch truck. Kaedon, Rylor, Jessie and Zane, rode in Kaedon's large truck with the four-wheel drive engaged. The road was treacherous in spots and became the focus of discussion between the brothers.

"Something's going to have to be done about this access," Rylor commented.

"We'll just need to make sure it's plowed routinely throughout the entire winter. The good news is this road is private and we could even automate the gate at the bottom to add another layer of protection," Kaedon suggested.

Jessie looked at the snow-covered terrain and then asked, "This used to be a logging camp?"

"Yes, about five years ago."

"How did the trucks and people living up here get to the property if this is the only road in?"

Rylor turned in the seat to face her, "It's not the only road in, but the only serviced road. There are several dirt roads that require four-wheel drives to navigate and are only passable during the summer months. The logging company didn't operate during the winter. They usually shutdown at the first sign of snow and didn't open back up until the roads had dried out, sometime in early May or late April."

"That makes me wonder whether or not the buildings are properly weather proofed. If the buildings aren't properly insulated and weren't winterized adequately, we could be looking at broken pipes and damaged ceilings. Have you been up here to actually see the property," Kaedon asked.

"About nine months ago I drove up here and looked around. I couldn't actually get inside the buildings, but I don't remember seeing any roof damage."

"That's good. Let's hope that's still the case."

Jessie was watching out the window, talking softly to Zane, when she caught a glimpse of blue metal roofs through the trees. "There it is," she called out, a strange excitement infusing her body. "Look, Zane. There's an eagle."

"There was a nesting pair of bald eagles down by the river the last time I was here. I saw them taking turns hunting and guarding the nest."

"They probably had eggs or babies inside," Kaedon told him.

"That's what I thought."

The vehicle started down the mountainside that led to the parking area in front of the largest of the buildings. They were constructed of brick and natural wooden logs supported the porches on the buildings that Jessie could see. Snow had drifted up against the sides of the buildings and large icicles hung from the metal roofing.

All of the structures had a blue metal roof and there were only a few areas that still had fencing upright. Jessie could imagine what this little piece of the mountain would look like in the spring when all of the grasses were new and the flowers were blooming.

"Here we are. I'd like to take a look at each building and maybe everyone can brainstorm what each one should be used for?" Rylor commented, getting out of the vehicle and gesturing for his parents to join them.

They headed into the first building. Rylor opened the door and he located the lights, pleased that the electricity had been turned back on. A large foyer greeted them and they split up to explore. Zane had adopted Rylor's parents and he held onto their hands and chattered away as they headed off to the right. She followed Rylor and Kaedon, noticing that they were both taking notes and pictures with their phones as they went.

"What can I do?" Jessie asked, wanting to help.

Kaedon handed her the tablet and pen in his hands with a smile. "You take notes."

Jessie nodded and did her best to jot down everything Kaedon was saying. This pattern continued as they explored the next five buildings. A total of a dozen buildings were included with the property, but three of them were nothing more than steel shells of buildings used to store logging equipment.

"What's happening with all of the equipment?" Kaedon asked, having a hard time believing that anyone had left this much equipment to just sit here and rot year after year.

"The owner told he sold it to a Canadian company who is planning to come and take it away the first part of March."

"Good, we'll need it out of our way before we start the heavy renovations. I think I've seen enough. Let's head back to the house. I want to put some numbers together this afternoon," Kaedon suggested a few hours later.

"Sounds good to me," Susan agreed. "This young man is

ready for lunch."

"Mommy, look what I found," Zane told her, holding out his hand to show her a little toy car that had definitely seen better days. The paint was chipped, and one tire was missing; and yet her little boy didn't care. It was a treasure that he'd found, and he was thrilled with it.

"That's a cool car, Zane. Why don't you put it in your pocket and when we get back to Susan's house, we'll wash it off?"

Zane smiled at her and made a big production of tucking it down into the front pocket of his overalls. Jessie patted him on the head and then spoke to Dakota and Susan, "Thanks for watching him while we all explored. I know he can be a handful."

"He was fine and so inquisitive. It was a pleasure to have him with us."

"Let's get out of here," Rylor said, waiting for everyone to exit before locking up the building.

They were headed back around the mountain when Rylor's phone rang. He answered it and Jessie could tell from the change in his voice that the news wasn't good. He was still on the phone when Kaedon's phone rang. Two calls inside of two minutes couldn't be good news.

Chapter 19

"It's Tom," Kaedon explained, pulling the truck over and answering the call. Jessie listened and felt herself go from relaxed to afraid in a matter of minutes. They both hung up their phones at the same time.

"What did Tom want?" Rylor asked before Jessie could voice her own question.

"Tom just called to tell me the Cheyenne police have issued a search warrant for a hotel room registered to one of Dino's goons. They also stated that Dino flew back into Cheyenne a few days ago. He's back in Wyoming. They've been looking for the black suburban all day and haven't found it. Cheyenne isn't that big."

Jessie felt her heart stall and then start beating rapidly again. "Dino's back to find me."

"That's what it looks like. His guys have been canvassing the gas stations and truck stops, flashing wads of money around and asking for a glimpse of the video surveillance tapes. I'm sorry to report that money talks and most of the business owners have given them access to the tapes."

Jessie nodded, "Did they visit the truck stop at the edge of town?"

"Yeah, they did," Kaedon told her.

"Then we can assume Dino probably knows where I am, or at least what direction I went."

"That's right."

"Well, I hate to add more worries, but that was Trevor on the phone. The feds in California have been gathering intel on Dino's warehouses and they watched three trucks pull into the compound yesterday and a few hours later they left. There was dark sedan following them and they're almost positive the passenger was Raul Suarez."

"Raul would only come to the states if there was a problem," Jessie murmured. "I remember Dino's dad talking about him once and Dominic... well, there was a fair amount of caution in his voice when he said Raul's name."

"Raul Suarez operates one of the largest drug cartels in South America. He almost never leaves Colombia, so if he made a personal trip up to see Dino, there's trouble brewing. Trevor's connections in California were able to get search warrants for all of the properties held by Salvatori Enterprises and their front companies. They also obtained wire taps and clearance to put the distribution center you visited under twenty-four-hour surveillance. Because Dino is not currently in California, they've elected to watch and wait."

"What are they going to do about Dino?" Jessie asked, trying to keep the fear from her voice. She glanced at Zane and he was happily watching a video on the tablet Susan had lent him. The bright green headphones kept him from hearing their conversation and for that, Jessie was very thankful.

"There's not much they can do until he breaks a law. They did obtain the license number and have put out a multi-state APB for the vehicle. Every federal, state, and local law enforcement agency is watching for him now."

Jessie's mind was whirling with all of the things that could go wrong while waiting. She had started to feel a measure of peace the last few days and was unwilling to lose that if she could possibly hold onto it.

"There's more," Rylor's voice broke into her thoughts.

"More?"

"According to Trevor's California counterpart, Raul Suarez hasn't left the country. They're not sure why he's still here and they haven't found him yet, but they've been monitoring the border closely and he hasn't been spotted."

"He could have flown or left by boat…"

"No. According to an expert on Raul Suarez, the man doesn't fly and won't step foot on a boat because he can't swim."

Kaedon chuckled, "It's nice to know that the leader of the world's most dangerous cartel is afraid of water and airplanes."

Suddenly, all three of them started laughing and were still trying to get themselves back under control when they arrived at the Ballard house. Dakota opened the door on Zane's side and then stared at them, "What on earth?"

"Dino came back to Cheyenne," Rylor informed his dad as tears of laughter ran down his cheeks.

"I fail to see the hilarity in that statement," Dakota informed them.

"It's okay, dad. Call it stress overload or something like that," Kaedon said, being the first one to regain control of himself.

"I'm taking Zane inside for lunch. I suggest you all contain yourselves before you enter the house or you'll be explaining things to your mother. And Jerricha called while we were driving back and has a song she wants you all to hear."

"A song? For Freedom Ranch?" Jessie asked.

"Once she gets a thought in her head, it's like a thorn she just can't get rid of until she gets the song finished. Let's get inside," Kaedon told her.

"You two go ahead. I'm going to call my office and let them

know I'm taking the rest of my vacation time now."

"Can you do that?" Jessie asked. "Won't you get in trouble?"

Rylor shook his head, "I turned in my two weeks' notice last week."

"You quit?" Jessie asked.

"I had to. I need to be here to get the safe house up and running…"

"I just didn't realize you were going to be quitting so soon," Jessie told him, her thoughts turning to where that might leave her. Rylor no longer was going to be her case worker and that meant she wouldn't be able to ask him for help when she left Warm Springs.

"Jessica, are you okay?" Kaedon asked.

"I'm fine. I am a bit tired… maybe I'll lie down with Zane after lunch. I'll go help your mother get it fixed." She slid from the truck and headed into the house, her mind racing with old fears once again. Dino had come looking for her and Rylor was no longer going to be there to support her in Cheyenne. She couldn't go back to her old apartment, not after hearing that Dino's goons had been watching it. *Maybe I should find a new place to live. I wonder what Colorado is like?*

Chapter 20

The rest of the day was spent watching Rylor make various phone calls and Kaedon play with a design program on his computer. Jerricha promised to share her song with them after dinner that evening, as she had promised Logan to meet him for lunch in town. Jessie did get Zane down for a brief nap, but she was unable to turn her mind off long enough to actually fall asleep. Susan seemed to sense her unease and suggested that she and Zane take a walk with her. Since the sun was shining overhead, Jessie bundled Zane into his winter coat and boots and they set out.

The mountain the Ballard's lived on was gorgeous, even covered in snow. "This place is amazing. You can see for miles up here," Jessie commented, looking out at the mountains and flatlands in the distance.

"I can't imagine living anywhere else," Susan told her with a warm smile. "Do you mind if I ask you a few questions?"

Jessie shook her head, "Not at all." Jessie was slowly getting to know a bit more about Susan Ballard and made a mental note to remind Rylor how lucky he was to have been born into such a caring family. She felt privileged to have even been a part of their family dynamic for just a few days. This was the type of home she wanted to create for herself and her son. The type of life she'd always dreamed of finding with each new foster home.

"There's a bench up here, just around this bend in the trail. Dakota and the kids put it up here years ago so that I could sit here and enjoy my quiet time." She glanced at Zane who had picked up an ice-covered stick and was taking great joy in smacking it against each tree or exposed rock. "You won't know what quiet time is for a few years yet, but when Zane is in school all day long and you have a few hours off, you'll find yourself sitting in a chair, staring at a blank wall, and it will be the best fifteen minutes of the day."

Jessie laughed, "I don't think that day will ever come. Not for me, anyway. Maybe it's easier for people who are married, but for most of my life, I've been on my own. The only time I ever felt like I could relax and be a kid was when I lived with the Jensen's. They hated that I knew how to do laundry and keep house at the age of ten. They were always encouraging me to go outside and play, but I didn't make friends easily and I wouldn't have known how to. Play, that is.

"While other little girls were playing dress up, school teacher, or doctor, I was struggling to get enough to eat and hoping I wouldn't get in trouble and punished for something I hadn't done."

Jessie looked over at Susan and saw tears in her eyes, "I'm sorry. I didn't mean to make you cry."

"Oh, sweetie. The fact that you not only survived your childhood, but living on the street, getting mixed up with a very bad man, and managed to have a baby at the age of eighteen and provide for him as well as you have... My tears are for the childhood you never got to experience, but also for the brave young woman you've become."

"I'm not brave," Jessie told her. "I'm scared all of the time."

"Bravery doesn't mean you never feel fear, it simply means you're willing to face what scares you and deal with it. Bravery is calling the man who is stalking you and trying to find a way to get him to stop. Bravery is talking to the FBI when you know your name is going to show up on the court order and that Dino will know it was you who sent the feds to his door."

"I didn't really have a choice about those things..."

"Didn't you? Think about it. When you first came here, the

night of Jerricha and Logan's wedding, you were planning to run. I could see it in your eyes. But you're still here. You're giving the system and the boys a chance to fix things."

"I was planning to take Zane and hitchhike to the East Coast. I thought maybe I could change my name and we'd be far enough away that Dino wouldn't be able to find us."

"What made you stay?" Susan asked her. They had reached the bench and she dusted off the snow before taking a seat.

Jessie dusted off the other end of the bench and sat down, looking out over the landscape as she thought about Susan's question. "I guess... hope. Somehow, Rylor managed to instill a little glimmer of hope inside of me, and Kaedon... there's something about him... I don't know how to explain it..."

"Attraction?" Susan offered.

Jessie glanced away from her and shrugged, "Maybe. To be honest, the only relationship I've ever had was with Dino and that was a complete sham. He didn't want a girlfriend or a wife, he wanted a pretty puppet that would jump at his command."

"Don't think about him right now," Susan advised her.

"I... I don't really trust myself, you know? I mean, I haven't got a great track record for making good decisions. I saw Kaedon with Marilee the other day and they seemed to be so in tune with one another. Like they knew what the other one was thinking before they said it."

Susan nodded, "That comes with knowing someone for a long time. Marilee and Kaedon grew up together. They were in the church nursery together, they were in the same school together. And Tom, her older brother, is Kaedon's best friend."

"But I thought she'd been gone for a long time?"

"She has been, but when you know someone, truly know

them, that doesn't just go away. Dakota and I have been married for thirty-five years this coming October. We finish one another's sentences and can communicate with just a look, but we didn't start out that way. It took time and effort on our parts."

"I hope I can find what you have one day."

"Tell me about your schooling. Rylor said you were taking some classes at the technical college."

"I'm pretty good at math and they offer this one-year program that teaches you how to be a bookkeeper. I thought maybe I could get a job doing that once Zane goes to school."

"That's a thought. Have you thought about where you might want to live?"

Jessie shook her head, "I'd planned to stay in Cheyenne, but I guess deep down I never really thought that would happen. I didn't make any friends, not even with the people I worked with."

"You don't seem to be having trouble making friends here. I've talked to several people who couldn't say enough about how sweet you were and what a good mother you were to Zane."

"These people don't really know me."

"And whose fault is that?" Susan asked. "Zane, are you ready to go back?"

"My hands are wet," he held out his snow-caked gloves and Jessie could see that snow had fallen down inside of them.

"Come here and let's take them off. You can put mine on until we get back to the house." Jessie removed his sodden gloves and then replaced them with her skin-warmed ones. "There, all better?"

Zane nodded and then wrapped his little arms around her neck, "Carry me."

"Always," Jessie told him. She picked him up, snuggled him close to her chest and then she caught Susan watching them.

"Sweetie, you are stronger than you know, and you have a mother's heart. No matter what this life has thrown at you, you've kept what's truly important in front of you. That little bundle of energy in your arms is your legacy and all the proof anyone needs of your character. Your past doesn't define you."

Jessie hugged Zane close and let Susan's words of affirmation repeat in her head as they walked back to the house. They arrived just as Kaedon was getting ready to head to town. Zane had fallen back asleep during their walk and Rylor took him from her arms and carried him to the guest bedroom.

Jessie looked at Kaedon and asked, "Are you going to the auditorium?"

"No. I'm going to see Marilee."

Jessie nodded and dropped her gaze. She knew Kaedon had said there was nothing romantic between them, but she still felt jealousy rise up in her chest. She moved to go around him when he reached out and snagged her arm. She looked up at him. "What?"

"Come with me," Kaedon suggested.

"To visit your old girlfriend?" Jessie said before she could push the words down.

"I won't deny that at one point we meant the world to one another, but that is not the case now. Come with me and meet her for yourself. You tried to help me understand the choices she's making. Let's see if you still feel the same way after talking to her in person."

Jessie searched his eyes and then nodded, "Fine. Let me see if Rylor…"

"I'll keep an eye on Zane," Dakota told her from the porch. "Go with Kaedon."

Jessie nodded and could have sworn she heard his dad murmur behind her, "He needs a friend right now and so do you."

Jessie sat quietly as Kaedon drove them into town. They arrived at Tom's house and Marilee opened the door with a smile for them both. "Come in. Tom's still at the office."

"I wanted to stop and see how things were going. Are you feeling alright?"

"I have good days and bad days. Jessie it's nice to see you again."

"I'm sorry to hear about your diagnosis."

"You've had experience with someone who died from cancer?"

"Yes. A foster mom when I was ten. The social workers removed me before she got really bad, but they took me to visit her once a week. Sometimes I wish I didn't have those memories of how sick she was."

"You understand why I want to go to Switzerland?" Marilee asked.

"I understand why you think it's a good idea, but I just wonder, did you bother to ask Tom and Kaedon what they want?"

Jessie saw Kaedon watching their exchange. "I did not ask them because they are not the ones who have to go through the end of this illness. I do. I freely admit I do not like pain and do not tolerate it graciously. You think there is something to be gained from me suffering unbearable pain?"

"Not at all. I completely agree with wanting to avoid pain that has no positive outcome. Unlike the pain of childbirth that results in a new life being born, the pain of dying from cancer only serves to humiliate and destroy the memories of a life well-lived. I think you are missing the fact that Tom and Kaedon would have liked to have a say. To be included."

Kaedon spoke up, "Marilee, the thought of you suffering for no reason makes me want to punch something. Neither Tom nor I want that."

Marilee looked at him and then held up her hands, "So what do you want? I made a decision that I was comfortable with. I need you to trust in my ability to choose the best end I can for my life."

"But you're cutting Tom and me out of the process."

"Why Switzerland?" Jessie interjected. "Isn't there someplace closer?"

Marilee shook her head, "I'm afraid not. Assisted suicide is only legal in a few places and then only if I would be able to give myself the injection. I want to live as long as can. Only Switzerland provides me a place to do that."

"Would you let Tom or Kaedon visit you or be with you at the end?"

"To what end?" Marilee asked.

"Well, just like you don't want to suffer, it's possible that Tom and Kaedon both need to deal with your impending death in a way that makes sense to them. Tom is your brother. He might want to be there to hold your hand and to ensure that your wishes are being carried out."

Marilee was quiet for a long moment and then she slowly nodded. "If they felt so strongly about being with me then, yes, I would be okay with them coming to Switzerland." She gave Kaedon a sad smile and then pushed herself to her feet, "I'm sorry to cut your visit short, but I tire so easily. Please, see yourselves out. Thank you for coming."

Jessie sat there, watching Kaedon as he tried to process things. "Did I overstep?" she finally asked.

Kaedon looked at her and then moved closer and tipped her chin up, kissing her gently before whispering against her lips, "Thank you... for trying to get me to see her perspective."

Jessie raised a hand and touched her lips, "Why did you do that?"

"Because it felt right. I've wanted to do that for a while now and it simply felt right."

"Okay."

"Okay. Let's get out of here."

Chapter 21

Middle of February...

Kaedon came into the house after having put in a full day of working on the auditorium. There were only a few things left to do, including re-upholstering the chairs that went in the balcony boxes. The fabric he had picked out had arrived several weeks earlier, but he'd been in no hurry to get it installed.

Jerricha was sitting on the couch with her guitar and he paused to listen for a moment before making his arrival known. "Sounds good, sis."

"Hey, Kaedon. Did you get my message?" Jerricha asked, looking around him and frowning when she saw he was alone. "Where's Jessie?"

Kaedon paused and then gave her a confused look, "I left her here with Zane this morning. Where do you think she is?"

"With you. Rylor had to drive back to Cheyenne to sign the paperwork for the transfer of the logging company and she wanted to visit Marilee. He dropped her and Zane off there three hours ago. I called and left a message on your voicemail."

Kaedon pulled his phone out, listened to his voice message and clenched his jaw. He tried to call Tom's house, but no one answered. "I'm heading back to town right now." He jumped back in his truck and then called Tom, "Where are you?"

"I'm in Drummond. Why?"

"Rylor dropped Jessie and Zane off at your house on his way

back to Cheyenne."

"What?"

"Yeah. Jerricha called and left me a message but I didn't get it until I got back to the house. I called your house and Marilee didn't answer."

"I'm headed back right now but it'll take me forty-five minutes at least. I'll call her cell phone and then call you back."

"I'm headed into town right now. I've got a bad feeling about this."

"Don't borrow trouble," Tom advised him.

Kaedon blew his breath out and then agreed, "Okay. I'll call you when I get there."

He disconnected the call and pushed his truck as much as he dared down the mountain. The weather had given way to days full of sunshine and the road was mostly dry now. He slowed down a bit as he reached Main Street, anxious to reach Tom's house on the outskirts. He arrived and saw Marilee's car in the driveway, but the front door was closed.

He parked on the street and then exited his truck, grabbing the crowbar from the back as he rounded the tailgate. He cautiously approached the front door, glancing in the front windows and seeing nobody inside. He rang the doorbell and then listened for movement, growing even more alarmed when the house remained eerily quiet.

He rounded the corner of the house, went to the back door and tried the handle, alarmed when it turned in his palm. He pushed it open and called out, "Marilee! Jessica! Where are you?"

No answers came back and Kaedon hesitantly entered the house. An examination of the first floor yielded no evidence of the three people he was searching for. "Jessica, where in tarnation are you?"

He called Tom back, "I'm at your house and no one is here."

"Did you go inside?"

"Yes, and again, there's no sign of either Marilee or Jessica. Where could they have gone? Marilee's car is in the driveway. Could they have walked into town?"

"I don't think so. Marilee has been really tired lately. She can barely make it up the stairs to her bedroom. I'm thinking of moving her things down to the guest suite this weekend."

"Where can they be? Did you try Marilee's cellphone?"

"It's going straight to voicemail, so it's either completely dead or she has the volume turned off. Take a look around the house. I should be there in ten minutes."

"What happened to forty-five?" Kaedon asked with a laugh in his voice.

"That's what sirens are for," Tom told him in all seriousness. "See you in a few minutes."

Kaedon hung up the phone and then headed outside. He checked the closest corral but there was no evidence of the women. The barn doors were closed and he headed in that direction, praying that they were in there and just hadn't been able to hear him.

He pulled the doors open, "Marilee! Jessie! Where are you?"

He walked further into the large barn and then he heard the faint sound of a little boy's giggle. It was the sweetest sound he'd ever heard, but even though he walked through the entire barn, he couldn't find the source of the noise. "Zane?" he called out.

The sound of Tom's siren came from the driveway. Kaedon met him in the yard, "I can hear Zane giggling, but there's no one in the barn. I've looked everywhere."

Tom gave him a puzzled look and then entered the barn

himself, listening for several minutes before the giggling sound reached his ears. A smile spread across his face and he strode for the rear of the barn. "This way. I'd forgotten about the tunnels."

"Tunnels?" Kaedon asked.

"The tunnels the outlaws used a hundred years and more ago. There are several of them beneath the barn. The entrance is beneath the silo."

"Why have I never heard about these tunnels?" Kaedon demanded to know

"Because my father threatened us within an inch of our lives if we said anything. He didn't want teenagers sneaking onto the property and getting lost or injured."

"How extensive are these tunnels?"

"Not very big. Mostly just a big cavern. Here, watch your step," Tom told him, descending into the bottom of the silo with confidence.

Kaedon followed him, thankful that Tom had a flashlight attached to his tool belt and wishing he had one of his own. He reached the bottom of the ladder and turned, stunned at the sight before him.

"Tom! Kaedon? What are you doing here?" Marilee asked.

"I think that is a question better answered by you," Tom told her. "You've had poor Kaedon here worried that something had happened to Jessie."

"I'm here and I'm fine."

"Jessica, I was supposed to pick you and Zane up hours ago. I didn't get the message until I was already up the mountain and then I couldn't raise anyone on the phone. The house was empty... the barn was empty..."

"How did you find us?" Marilee asked.

"Zane's giggles echoed upwards."

At the mention of his name, Zane lifted his head and then rushed at Kaedon, "Come and help me build."

Kaedon picked him up and murmured in his ear for a moment before turning his gaze back to the women. "Jessica, we need to head back to the house. Trevor called me a few hours ago and is supposed to be here in," he consulted his watch. "Forty minutes."

"Trevor is coming to see me? What about Rylor? He went back to Cheyenne."

"Yes, but he's driving back tonight." Kaedon turned his gaze to the other woman. "Marilee, how are you feeling?"

"Tired. Nauseous. Weak. I'm leaving for Switzerland in two weeks."

Tom looked upset to hear this but Kaedon wasn't going to get involved in this struggle. "I'll call you later."

"Jessica, let's go," Kaedon indicated for her to climb the ladder ahead of him. Once they were back on the ground level, she turned on him.

"Arc you mad at me?"

"Not mad, just concerned because we couldn't find you and I started thinking the worst had happened. It wasn't a pleasant feeling."

She gazed at him and asked, "Why not?"

"Do you really want to have this discussion here, with your son present?"

"Why not?" Jessie asked again.

Kaedon strode towards his truck, securing Zane into the safety seat in back and then turning to see that she had followed him a short distance. "Why not? Maybe because no matter how hard I try to deny it, I'm developing feelings for you. That's why not?"

"You don't want to have feelings for me," Jessie surmised.

"It's not just you. I don't want to have these feelings for anyone."

Jessie gave him a sad look and then climbed into the truck, "We should go."

Kaedon paced outside the truck for a moment and then tossed the keys in her direction. "I'm going to walk some of this negative energy off. Take my truck and I'll catch a ride back home."

"I can't," Jessie told him, holding the keys gingerly and as if they might break.

"Can't or won't?" Kaedon asked.

"Can't. I can't drive. I don't know how."

Kaedon was taken aback, "You don't know how to drive?"

"No."

"So how have you been getting around?"

"Either one of you takes me or I walk. I'm used to it so it's no problem."

"It is a problem. You need to know how to drive, especially living up on the mountain."

Jessie shook her head, "But I don't live up on the mountain. You do. I'm just visiting."

Kaedon glanced at the truck to see that Zane's adventures in the tunnels had worn him out and he was more than half asleep. "You and I need to talk. Let's take Zane up to the house and then you and I are going to take a drive."

Jessie watched him and then slowly nodded her head and

silently climbed into the truck. She was quiet all the way home. "Sit tight and I'll be right back," Kaedon told her.

He removed the sleeping little boy from the safety seat and handed him off to Jerricha. "We're going to take a drive and get some things settled. We'll be back in a while."

"Zane will be safe with me. Good luck. She's strung tight and each day her fear is taking a larger hold on her spirit."

"I know. I'm going to get to the bottom of it now."

Chapter 22

Kaedon drove the truck towards the site of the new safe house and then he parked and cut the engine, turning to face her on the seat. "Okay, let's hear it."

"What are you talking about?" Jessie asked.

"Jessica, for the past few weeks you have been withdrawing and I want to know what's going on in your brain to cause such a drastic change."

"I don't know what you expect. I've been here for over a month now and I'm no closer to being able to get on with my life than before. I hate this living in limbo. I'm afraid to make friends because I'll just have to leave them when Dino gets close again. Zane is growing up before my eyes and needs a stable home, but I can't give that to him while Dino is hunting me. I probably have a target on my back because I let my name be used on the search warrants. And to my knowledge, those haven't even been served.

"And in case you missed it, I'm complaining. Loudly. This isn't living."

"Jessica, I understand your frustration, but you are safe here. I didn't realize, I don't think any of us did, that you weren't feeling accepted here."

"That's not it," Jessie argued. "Everyone has gone out of their way to make me feel included. I've never felt so at home, but it's all an illusion. This is your home, not mine."

"You said that earlier. Have we done something to make you feel less than welcome?"

"You know you haven't," Jessie told him softly. "I just..."

143

Kaedon reached across the truck's bench seat and pulled her towards him, "You just what? Don't like living in Warm Springs?"

"I love it here. The townspeople are so warm and friendly."

"Then it's the size of the town. Too small?"

"I hate big cities. They are easy to get lost in but I always felt confused and like I didn't know which way to go."

"Kaedon, you can't understand this because you've always had a family. You've always had a place to call home and you knew it would be there when you woke up. At any time, word could come that Dino is headed this way and I will have to pack what I can and leave. It's exhausting living like this."

"Do you believe the authorities are working on taking Dino down?"

"I want to believe that, but I haven't seen it."

"Do you enjoy spending time with me? Do you believe that I would do anything to help keep you and Zane safe?" Kaedon asked into the silence of the truck.

Jessie looked at him, "I believe you would keep us safe… you know I enjoy spending time helping you on the auditorium…"

"That's not what I asked you," Kaedon reminded her.

"I… I don't understand what you are asking me." Jessie was feeling very flustered.

"Don't you? You told me many weeks ago that you felt nothing for my brother. I want to know what you feel for me. Do you see me as just a brother or as someone who could become more?"

"You're asking me questions I don't know how to answer. I do like being with you. I feel safe and… I don't see you as a brother. Is that what you want to hear? I find myself wondering about things that I know will only lead to heartache because I cannot stay here. I cannot endanger everyone who has tried to help me by staying."

"We can take care of ourselves. We can take care of you. I can take care of you.

It grew silent in the truck. "I have an idea," she leaned towards him. "What if I called Dino again to offer my condolences on his father's death? Maybe I could figure out why he came back here…"

"That's a bad idea. The feds are building their case. They don't want Dino getting off on any technicality."

"But Rylor said Raul Suarez might have slipped back into Colombia without anyone seeing."

"That's a possibility. Trevor is coming by to talk to you in a few minutes. Let's hear what he has to say and then we can discuss this further. Okay?"

"Fine," Jessie relented. She'd always liked Trevor and hopefully he'd be able to tell her something she could use.

Kaedon gave her a smile, "That's all I can ask for. Trevor is meeting with us at the diner. I didn't want him coming up to the house and possibly upsetting Zane."

"But, what about Maggie and her propensity to gossip?"

"You and Zane have been here a month now and this won't be the first time Maggie has seen you. Almost everyone attends church services on Sundays and you've been to several of those already."

Kaedon drove them to the diner just in time to grab a booth and meet with Trevor.

"So, there's been a few developments I thought you should know about. First, there is an all-out war happening in San Francisco."

"What does that mean?"

"It means that the Salvatori cartel is being systematically torn apart by rival groups. Raul Suarez did return to Colombia, but only to amass more fire power. A few days ago, another exchange was to take place. Three trucks arrived at the distribution docks, but instead of them containing pallets of drugs, they were loaded with armed South American drug cartel members. It was a blood bath.

"The Korean mafia was waiting on the other side, ready to take out anyone who thought to escape."

"And Dino?"

"They haven't identified him as being one of the killed. They're positive he was there when the trucks arrived..."

"How are they sure of that?" Kaedon inquired.

"They managed to get someone on the inside. Undercover. Agents were waiting to take the trucks after they picked up the girls. They did so about three miles down the road. Two dozen young girls between the ages of eleven and nineteen were rescued and returned to their families."

"But they don't know what happened to Dino?"

"No. The undercover agent had managed to get close to Dino and thinks there is a good possibility he's trying to find you. You should know, he received a photograph last week showing you at a store in Drummond. That's probably where he's headed."

"Drummond isn't that big. If Dino starts showing her picture around, people will send him here."

"Then we just have to be ready for him. From here on out, you don't go anywhere with at least one man with you, I'd prefer two. Dino is a desperate man right now. His family enterprise is completely dismantled. His brother was killed during the raid, so he is now all alone. He's going to blame you for this."

"Stop trying to scare her," Kaedon warned Trevor.

"I'm not trying to scare her, I'm just trying to make sure she understands the stakes have increased dramatically. Dino is a man with nothing to lose. That makes him completely unpredictable and the worst sort of criminal to stop."

"I'm taking her back to the mountain and she's not leaving until this psycho is caught. We're closing the gate access, as well."

"That sounds like a good idea. I have eight agents coming in tonight and we'll be stationing them throughout Warm Springs and they will also rotate standing guard at the house itself. We're going to get this man sooner or later."

"Make it sooner, please."

Trevor nodded, squeezed her shoulder and then left the diner. Jessie didn't realize she was shaking until Kaedon took her hands in his own and began to chafe them.

"Hey! Settle down. Jessica, look at me." He waited until she did so and then he pulled her into his arms while she broke down and cried. Jessie tried to stop herself, but it was all too much.

"He's coming for me."

"But he's not going to get to you. Come on, let's get out of here. Maggie will understand if we don't stay and eat. She was eavesdropping the entire time."

Kaedon pulled her from the booth and wrapped a comforting arm around her shoulders. He stopped and warned Maggie, "Pretend you didn't just hear all of that. You didn't see Jessie and you don't know who she is. Got it?"

"Yes. I'll spread the word…"

"Fine, but do it in person. No social media. None."

"Got it. Jessie, you'll be fine. You just let Kaedon take care of you. He's one of the good guys. It's the only kind we raise up around here."

Jessie nodded and tended to agree. So far, the only men she'd met who had been born and raised in Warm Springs were indeed good men. Kind. Compassionate. Strong in character and convictions. Trustworthy. All of the things that made a man a good friend. *Did those same qualities also hold true for romantic relationships?*

Chapter 23

The next day...

"I hate sitting here," Jessie murmured to no one and everyone.

Susan and Jerricha had both elected to stick close to the house and help keep Zane amused. Jerricha was currently sitting on the opposite couch with her guitar in her hands and Zane sitting adoringly at her feet.

"He likes you," Jessie told her.

"He has good taste," Jerricha fired back. "So, I haven't had a chance to play the song I wrote for Freedom Ranch for Rylor. Is he coming back today?"

"I don't know. Kaedon was going to call him last night but I forgot to ask him if he did so. I'm worried that Rylor won't know what's happening. Trevor couldn't get ahold of him."

"I'm sure he'll call when he can."

Susan and Dakota came back into the living room and settled on the sofa. "Zane, would you like to beat me at a game of checkers," Dakota asked.

Jessie smiled as she watched them all interacting. Susan and Dakota treated Zane as if he were their grandchild and Jessie felt a stab of pain that she'd never be able to let him meet her own parents.

"What's putting that sad look on your face?" Jerricha asked softly for her ears only.

"Just thinking about what can't be."

Jerricha shook her head and then slipped from the couch, carrying her guitar in one hand and pulling Jessie along behind her with the other. "We'll be down for lunch."

"Where are we going?" Jessie whispered.

"Girl talk."

Jerricha pulled her into the bedroom she'd used as a young girl and sat her down on the bed. "Red, Orange, or Pink?"

Jessie was completely lost. "What?"

"Red, Orange, or Pink? I might have some purple around here also."

"Jerricha, what are you talking about?"

"Nail polish. Girl, have you never engaged in girl talk?"

Jessie shook her head, "I guess not."

"Wow! Just... wow. Okay, so we're going to polish each other's nails and share all of our secrets. It'll be fun."

"I don't think I have any secrets I really want to reveal," Jessie told her.

Jerricha produced a tray full of nail polish and then settled on the bed opposite Jessie. "I'll go first with the secret thing. Oh, I should reminded you that whatever we say up here, stays up here."

"Really? You wouldn't tell your husband what we discussed?"

"Not without gaining your permission. So, I want red on both of my fingers and my toes." Jerricha handed her the bottle of nail polish and then she settled back on the pillows.

"For my secret, I'm going to tell you something that not even Logan knows. At least, not until tonight. We're going to have a baby."

"Congratulations," Jessie told her, swiping one of Jerricha's toes with the polish. "How does a pregnancy fit in with your music career?"

"Well, this first year while I'm going out as a solo act, I'm just doing little weekend shows. Nothing too big. I was hoping that maybe you could give me some pointers?"

Jessie started shaking her head, "I didn't have a clue what I was doing with Zane. Truly, I just went from one thing to another. No forethought. No letting people take care of me. My best advice is sleep now. You won't get a goodnight's sleep after the baby comes for something like eighteen years."

Jerricha giggled and then wiggled her freshly painted toes in the air. "Good job. Now, your turn. What color?"

Jessie selected a deep pink color, "This one."

"Good choice. So, what kind of secret do you have?"

Jessie shook her head, "I don't really have any I want to share."

"Oh, come now. There has to be something you want to know or wish to share with me." Jessie watched her nails being painted and then grinned. "This has been fun."

"Sure has. Did you decide on something? Something you want to know?" Jerricha added.

"No."

"Well then, answer me a question. Why aren't you and Kaedon closer?"

Jessie swallowed audibly, "What do you mean by closer?"

"I mean, it's pretty obvious that you two like one another and yet, you still treat him like a stranger. If you're waiting for him to take the first step, you should probably be warned that might not work in this case. He's pretty pigheaded."

"So I've been warned. I just don't want to get hurt."

"Getting hurt is part of the process. Being willing to take a risk. I think you should go for it. In fact, you could plan a little dinner together with just the two of you."

"They don't want me leaving the house."

"Well, the barn isn't really…"

"The barn will afford you two some privacy. Go one, call Kaedon and tell him you want to talk to him tonight during dinner."

"What about Susan?"

"Susan is a diehard romantic at heart. If you explain what you're trying to do, she'll be more than willing to help put this together."

Jessie was quiet for a while. Wondering if Jerricha was right and she needed to take a leap of faith. Instead of hiding from her feelings for Kaedon, she needed to embrace them.

Their girl time over, Jerricha and Jessie went back downstairs to join the others, only to find that Rylor still hadn't returned and no one had been able to get ahold of him. Everyone was starting to get worried but there was nothing they could do but wait and hope he got his voice messages soon and called home.

Chapter 24

Drummond...

Dino was seething with anger and a hunger for revenge. Everything he and his family had worked for was now gone. First his father had died. The coroner had listed the cause of death a heart attack, but Dino knew better. She'd somehow found a way to get to his dad from several states away.

And then she'd managed to turn Raul Suarez against him. Dino shuddered as he recalled the terror he'd felt when the back of the trucks had flown up and dozens of South American young men armed with weapons he'd helped supply had rushed forward. They'd been prepared for a fight and had started shooting immediately. Dino had ducked out of the way as those around him were gunned down. Sam, Jimmy, and Tony... all dead.

Dino had panicked and rushed for the front of the building and his private parking lot, only to watch as the Korean mafia mowed down anyone thinking to escape Raul's justice. Cursing a blue streak, Dino took the stairs down to the sub-ground floor exit. His father had been paranoid and having multiple exits from every business and home had never been as important as it was that day.

He'd gotten into the black vehicle and emerged onto a public street several blocks away ten minutes later. Every cop in the city had been called to help deal with the situation and Dino had no trouble slipping from the city without drawing attention to himself.

The anonymous tip he'd gotten as to Jessie's location had been a sign and he'd set a course for its point of origin. Now he'd arrived and was a little depressed that Jessie wasn't a resident of the small town. Dino didn't have a picture to hand around, just one on his phone that had been taken the night of her seventeenth birthday. She was quite a few years older now, but Dino wasn't worried that she wouldn't look the same. Jessie possessed a timeless beauty.

He stopped at the gas station and inquired inside, "I'm looking for a young woman, name is Jessica."

The gas station attendant shook his head, "Don't know of anyone in Drummond by that name."

"Hmm, I was sure I was told I could find her around here."

"Well, there are quite a few small towns scattered north and west. I could draw you a map if you like."

"That would be very helpful. Thank you." Dino waited and then looked at the map. There were just three towns noted. Dino stared at the names and chose one to start with. It might take him an extra day, but he was committed to finding Jessie and making her pay for destroying his life.

He climbed back into the car and headed towards Warm Springs. It was less than an hour away, according to the map. He could afford to check the town out and if it wasn't the right one, he'd backtrack and choose another.

*****

Warm Springs...

Trevor and Tom both received the notification from the surveillance team at the same time. Tom had been spending more and more time with Marilee as her condition worsened. She was due to fly out of Cheyenne in two days' time for Switzerland. Tom wasn't completely on board with the idea of her dying all alone and was planning on flying out to join her at the end of April.

154

"I can't imagine how hard things must be for you right now," Trevor commiserated with him.

"It's hard. She asked me to drive her to the airport in Cheyenne and I can already tell you I'm going to cry all the way home. It could very well be the last time I see her."

"You still having problems with the assisted suicide concept?"

"Not so much any longer. In a lot of ways, it's a merciful way to deal with the disease that is cancer. She's already in so much pain some days… I hate knowing that there's nothing I can do to make it better."

"That would suck. Don't look now, but there's our boy."

Trevor and Tom waited until Dino parked his car in front of Maggie's Diner and went inside. Trevor gave the signal for the agents who were hiding to close in and keep the small diner surrounded. "He's not getting away this time."

Tom nodded and he and Trevor headed inside the diner. "Maggie, how are things going today?" he inquired politely.

"Tom, good enough. How's that sister of yours?"

"She's leaving soon. I'm telling everyone and you could help me pass it around, if they want to say goodbye, they should plan on stopping by the house tomorrow."

Maggie nodded and then patted him on the shoulder, "Of course I'll pass it along. Most of this town remembers her growing up. She'll be missed."

"That she will."

"So what can I get you two boys?"

"How about just some coffee for now?" Tom lowered his voice and Maggie dipped her head, "Best be getting everyone else out of here for now, as well. Agents are guarding the exits."

Maggie nodded, returned with two cups of coffee and then started moving everyone along. It was the middle of the afternoon and the dinner rush hadn't arrived yet.

Tom and Trevor waited until two of Trevor's men stepped into the kitchen and then it seemed like everything happened in slow motion. Tom and Trevor approached Dino's table at the same time he pulled out his gun and started firing.

Both men dove behind the nearest table, but the fight didn't last long. Dino hadn't seen the agents coming in from the rear. With one shot, Dino's life was over and the destruction he and his family had wrought on so many lives was finally at an end. Tom stood over the man's lifeless body while Trevor radioed for a cleanup crew to come to the diner.

"Well, he won't be causing any more harm."

Kaedon came striding into the diner, "What's going on over here? I was on my way home and saw all of the cars come to this point."

"Dino Salvatori is dead."

Kaedon looked at where the body lay and nodded once, "I'm headed home and I'll let everyone know. I was actually going to try and find you, Tom. Have you heard from Rylor? He should have been calling in hours ago. We're all starting to get a bit worried."

"I'll put out an APB for his vehicle between here and Cheyenne. Maybe he broke down in one of the dead zones?" Tom suggested.

"I hope it's something that simple. At least I can take the worry off the table that Dino had anything to do with his disappearance."

"We'll find him. Don't worry."

Chapter 25

Kaedon walked into the house and hollered for everyone to join him. Everyone was home today except for Logan and Rylor, but that didn't matter. They would find out for themselves.

"Dino is dead. He was shot and killed in the diner half an hour ago."

Jessie paused for only a moment and then flung herself into his arms, "It's over."

Kaedon wrapped her in his arms and placed a tender kiss on her hair. 'It's all over. You're free to live wherever and however you want."

Jessie was crying and wetting his shirt with her tears. "Sorry, but I didn't realize it would feel this way."

"Don't apologize for how you feel. It is what it is and you deserve to feel a sense of relief right now."

They all exchanged well wishes and then Susan excused herself to begin dinner. Jerricha and Dakota took Zane outside for a walk, leaving Kaedon and Jessie alone.

"Come sit with me," Kaedon urged her. He pulled her down next to him on the couch, threading their fingers together. "Talk to me. What are you thinking right now?"

Jessie nodded at him, "Guilt."

"For what?" Kaedon inquired.

"For feeling happiness when a man is dead. For knowing that I prayed for his death… it was kind of the only thing God and I had to talk about. He must think I'm a horrible person."

"God loves you and I think He probably is satisfied that justice has been served." Kaedon lifted a hand to her hair and smoothed it back softly, "Now that you no longer have to worry about Dino, can we discuss your feelings for me?"

Jessie looked up at him and then chuckled, "You're relentless."

"No, I just want to know where I stand. I have to leave for Colorado tomorrow. I have to go finish up the project I started before the snow fell."

"How long will you be gone?"

"A couple of weeks. Will you be here waiting for me when I return?"

"I... I don't know."

"You know mom and dad consider you part of the family and have no intention of letting you just waltz out of our lives. You and Zane belong here."

"We do?" Jessie asked, her mind a mixture of confusion with all that had happened.

"You do. I also have a job offer for you if you're interested."

"What?"

"Cooking at the school. Belle is retiring and they need someone to replace her with. You really impressed them the last few weeks. The job is yours if you want it."

"Can I think about it? I need to talk to Rylor..."

"What about?" Kaedon demanded. "What is it that you can talk to him about but not me?"

"You."

Kaedon looked at her and then chuckled derisively, "You

want to talk to Rylor about me?"

"He's my sounding board."

"Let me be that instead."

"Okay, well, see, there's this guy that I like. I'm pretty sure, no, I'm positive he likes me, too, but we're from two completely different worlds and backgrounds."

"Differences can be good."

"But they could also cause problems down the road."

"That's true as well. Are you ready to take a leap of faith where this guy is concerned?"

"That's my problem. I'm running a little low on faith right now."

"Do you trust this guy?" Kaedon asked softly, all pretense of being her sounding board suddenly gone. He was going to be gone for several weeks and he wanted to know now what he'd be coming home to.

"I do, now."

Kaedon cupped her face in his hands and held her gaze with his own, "Then trust in the love I have for you. Trust me to never hurt you or forsake you for another." Kaedon lowered his head and kissed her so tenderly, and then he deepened the kiss bringing her body flush with his own. After a long kiss, Kaedon broke away. "So, I was thinking that since you're going to be working here, possibly… and we have these feeling for one another, that maybe we should explore a future together, as well."

Jessie looked at him and sighed, "Please… can you wait for an answer? I just need some time to be free."

"As long as you promise me not to run, you can have all the time in the world." He kissed her one last time and then set her away from him. "Tom put out an APB on Rylor's vehicle. We'll find him and then a real celebration can begin."

*****

Rylor felt his feet slide in the gooey mud once more and he tried not to lose his patience. His business in Cheyenne hadn't taken very long at all and he'd decided to see what the backroad into the property looked like. He should have turned around and gone back when it first started getting rough, but he hadn't. He'd kept driving until the vehicle was impossibly stuck in the mud.

He'd tried to call for some assistance, but there was no cell service on this part of the mountain. That had left him the one option, and he'd taken off for the long walk home. It had now been close to five hours since he'd first gotten stuck and he could finally see the blue roofs of the logging buildings. Correction, after today, all of those buildings belonged to the Freedom Ranch.

"Of all days for this to happen. You should be at home celebrating closing on this property." Rylor kept up the dialogue with himself as he walked another mile. His shoes and pants were completely caked with drying mud, making each step he took seemed heavier and harder.

Rylor finally reached the buildings and sat down to rest for a minute or two. He was sitting there when the sound of helicopter rotors approaching reached his ears. He looked up and then stood up and started waving his arms overhead. It was one of the choppers from Rapid Falls and when the pilot started descending, Rylor knew they'd spotted him.

Rylor kept his distance while the pilot landed the small craft and then he ducked his head and rushed forward. "Thank you."

"Man, what are you doing all the way out here by yourself?"

"I tried to use the backroads into the old camp here. There was too much mud and I got stuck. No cell service."

"Yeah. I got a call from the sheriff over in Warm Springs to look for a guy with car trouble or some other emergency. Where to? Warm Springs?"

"Please." Rylor watched the landscape float by beneath the chopper and added several more things to his list of renovations. The first was either a satellite phone or a cell tower. The second was signs warning all travelers to avoid the backroad entrances. They were simply unsafe and there was no way of even knowing someone was stuck.

The pilot let him off on the football field of the high school and Rylor made his way inside, quickly locating Logan.

"What happened to you?" his brother-in-law demanded.

"I made a stupid decision. Can I get a ride up the mountain?"

"Sure. I was just getting ready to call it a day. So, how are the renovation plans coming along?" Logan asked as they headed towards the mountain road.

"Fine. Good. As soon as the roads dry out a bit more we'll be able to get in there and get things going."

"You sound excited."

"I am. Freedom Ranch is finally going to come to fruition and should be up and running before summer's end."

Chapter 26

Dinner that night was a very happy affair. Dakota and Susan were thrilled that everything seemed to be working out for their children.

"So, Jessie, are you going to take the job at the school?" Rylor asked.

"I think so. It won't start until fall…"

"Feel like helping me with the safe house project until then?" he asked with a grin.

"I'd love to."

"I wants to help," Zane spoke up.

"Little man, we'll find you something to help with."

"I wants a saw like Kaedon," Zane told everyone with an emphatic nod of his head.

"Hey, I thought we talked about working our way up to power tools?" Kaedon teased him.

"I think we need to buy this kid a set of plastic tools. Then he can go for it without the fear of injuring himself or others."

"I'm headed to Colorado," Jerricha mentioned. "I'll look for something there."

"What's in Colorado?" Rylor asked.

"Jerricha will be performing her debut solo concert to a sold out crowd at a small venue in Denver."

"That's cool, sis. I'm really happy for you," Rylor told her with a smile.

"Thanks. My band is going to be there... it's going to be strange not having them on stage with me."

Logan reached over and kissed her cheek before declaring, "You're going to kill it."

"So, what else are we celebrating here?" Jessie asked, winking at Jerricha.

Jerricha rolled her eyes and then stood up and got everyone's attention. "I have something we can celebrate. We're going to have a baby."

"Congratulations!"

"Oh, Jerricha. I'm so happy for you."

"A baby? Are we ready for a baby?" Logan whispered.

"You have approximately eight months to wrap your head around this news, husband of mine."

Logan nodded and then pulled Jerricha from her chair and led her towards the stairs, "We'll be back, don't wait to eat on our account."

Chuckles all around the table filled Jessie's heart with a sense of belonging and happiness like she'd never known before. She met Kaedon's eyes across the table and blushed.

"Well, this has been quite the day for this family."

"It sure has. I'm completely exhausted and am going to turn in early. Hey, Zane, wanna come watch a movie with me before bed?"

"Yay!" Zane climbed down from the table and raced towards Rylor's room.

Rylor gave his parents a conspiratorial look and then suggested, "Why don't you and Jessie go check out what's playing over in Drummond?"

Jessie looked at Kaedon and waited for him to respond. "We don't have to…"

"I know. Grab a jacket and let's go. We'll be home later."

The drive to Drummond was mostly accomplished in silence, like so many of their exchanges but tonight Jessie found it strangely uncomfortable. Kaedon finally started talking.

"Feel any better now than before?"

"Much. I think it was just the sudden shock of it all. I haven't felt this free in so long."

"That's good, Jessica. Real good."

"Can I ask you a question? Why do you always call me Jessica?"

Kaedon gave a small laugh and shook his head, "You really want to know?" When she nodded, he sighed, "Because my brother calls you Jessie. Besides, Jessica is so much refined sounding, just like you."

"I'm not refined," Jessie argued.

"But you are. Come over her," he patted the bench seat and she slid over. He placed her hand on his thigh and then covered her hand with his own. "I know I said I'd give you some time, but I was wondering…"

Jessie giggled, "It's only been a few hours. I was thinking a little more time than that."

Kaedon smirked and then nodded. "Well, the movie is about two and a half hours, will that be enough time?"

"For me to decide that what we have is worth exploring?" Jessie questioned.

"Yes. I want a future with you, Jessica."

"I already know the answer to that question and it's yes. I've never felt this way before and while that scares me, being away from you scares me more."

Kaedon pulled the truck over on the highway and then kissed her, deepening the kiss and pulling her close against him. "Jessica, I think I'm falling in love with you. When I get back from Colorado, we need to have a serious conversation about moving forward. I'm thirty years old and I know what I want." When she opened her mouth to answer him, he covered her lips with a finger, "Don't say anything now, just think about it. Think about me."

He kissed her one last time and then pulled the truck back onto the road and completed the drive to Drummond. They watched a silly comedy and then returned to Warm Springs.

One thought kept going through Jessie's head the entire night. *I could have this life. It could be everything I've ever dreamed it could.*

Chapter 27

One month later…

Jessie was more excited than she could ever remember being. Kaedon had finally finished up his restoration project in Colorado and was coming home today. Jerricha and Logan were back from another weekend concert and were discussing plans for the grand opening of Freedom Ranch to happen later this summer.

Zane was growing like a weed and had started attending a pre-Kindergarten class a few mornings a week, giving Jessie time to work in the school kitchen and learn as much as possible from Belle before she retired. The woman had postponed her retirement to the end of the school year to give Jessie time to learn as much as she could.

Rylor was loving overseeing the renovations of the buildings. Kaedon had been coming home every week to spend a day getting the construction crews lined out on what needed to happen next. It was still quite a ways out from being completed, but she'd never seen Rylor so happy.

The only dark spot in their lives had been Marilee's death. True to her wishes, the people taking care of her in Switzerland had kept Tom apprised of her condition. When things had gotten significantly worse, they'd notified him and he'd flown to Switzerland and been right by her side as she slipped away from the pain and destruction the cancer was wreaking on her body.

Tom had asked Kaedon to go with him, and while Jessie had encouraged him to do so, Kaedon hadn't felt comfortable with the request. Rylor had stepped up and gone with him, being a support system for Tom during the grieving process.

The town had held a memorial service for Marilee upon Tom's return with her ashes. It had been beautiful and a lasting tribute to a woman who'd shown extraordinary strength in the midst of trying circumstances. Jerricha had been present and had sung with the high school choir, bringing everyone to their knees in tears.

The sound of tires crunching in the driveway had Jessie up off the couch and out the door before anyone could say a word. She flew down the steps and was in Kaedon's arms before he could even fully alight from his vehicle.

"Whoa! What a reception."

"I missed you," Jessie replied, kissing him deeply.

When they broke apart, Kaedon tipped her chin up and asked, "I was just home a week ago. What's different today?"

"You don't have to leave again," Jessie told him, lifting herself up on her tiptoes and capturing his mouth in a deep kiss once more.

"Sure there's not anything else I'm missing?"

Jessie gave him a coy smile and murmured, "You're back and I've had plenty of time to think."

"Ah, the question."

Jessie nodded and then moved back so that Kaedon could get out of the truck. He grabbed her hand and pulled her towards the trail that led to the overlook bench. Like Susan, it had become her favorite place to meditate.

Kaedon didn't stop until they were standing on the overlook, the world spread out before them with signs of spring all around. Snow still lingered on the mountain tops but the valleys below were green and brimming with life.

167

Kaedon turned to her, digging in his pocket and removing a small black jewelers box. Jessie's eyes opened wide in surprise and he merely chuckled. He dropped to one knee and held the box out to her, "Jessica Niles, would you do me the pleasure of agreeing to become my wife?"

Jessie felt tears fill her eyes. This was what she'd been hoping for since Kaedon had first placed the thought in her head, but she'd held it at bay because it seemed too normal. Jessie had never done normal.

"Jessica, are you going to leave me hanging out here?" Kaedon asked her quietly, still holding up the black jeweler's box.

Jessie shook her head and picked up the box, opening it to reveal a gorgeous diamond solitaire with a silver band. The ring looked older and she raised a questioning brow.

"It was my grandmother's. I've been carrying that around in my pocket for what seems like forever. Even when I was in Colorado, I carried it with me as a reminder of what might be waiting for me back home."

Jessie sat down on the bench and Kaedon joined her, "After Dino… well, I never thought I'd have a chance to feel love or be loved… but you gave that back to me. Thank you. And yes, I would love to marry you."

Kaedon swept her body close to his own, sealing her agreement with a kiss. They continued to kiss for long moments until they were both out of breath.

"So, I've had lots of time to think," Kaedon told her. "About where we should live."

Jessie nodded, "I find I no longer care as long as it's with you. Where would you like to live?"

"I was thinking right here would be good. All of our family is here and I mean, our family. They are as much yours now as they are mine. You told me once that all you'd ever wanted was a family and a home. You better than anyone understand that it takes more than bodies and a building to make that happen.

"I want to build a home with you, Jessica. I want to have a family with you."

"I want those things too, but I've come to realize that a home can be anywhere as long as your heart is there with it."

"Ready to go share the news with everyone else?" Kaedon asked after a while.

"I think they already guessed. I've been waiting for you to get home all day."

Kaedon chuckled and then stood up, pulling her into the crook of his arm as they made their way back to the house. "I'd like to build us our own house, but it will have to wait until after the safe house opens. Can you wait until then?"

Jessie considered the options and smiled, "Let's get married at the safe house."

"That's the perfect idea. Let's go talk to Rylor and then you, my mom, and Jerricha can start making all of the plans you like."

Epilogue

Freedom Ranch, Warm Springs, Wyoming

Two months later…

Rylor tapped on the door to the room being used as the bride's dressing area and waited for his mother or sister to answer.

"Rylor, is it almost time?"

Rylor nodded and then stepped into the room, his eyes taking in the lovely vision standing before him. "Jessica you look absolutely amazing. Like a princess come to life."

"Thank you, kind sir. Are you here to escort me to where my prince awaits?"

Rylor executed a formal bow, "As you request, milady."

Susan hugged Jessie and then Jerricha did the same. "We're going to go find our seats. You look beautiful."

"Thank you both for everything. I've never felt so doted on before."

"It was our pleasure."

The door closed behind the two women and Rylor couldn't take his eyes off of her. "Kaedon better know how lucky he is," Rylor commented. "I'm so proud of you. Look how far you've come. You are my greatest success story and I owe your final transformation to the power of love and acceptance of self."

Jessie walked towards him, "Rylor, for the first time in my life, I like who I am. I'm still working through my past and probably always will be doing that to some degree, but I'm no longer letting it define me. You gave me that chance and I will never be able to thank you enough for it."

"I didn't do it for your thanks, I did it because I care about you. Now, ready to go get married?"

Jessie nodded and took his proffered elbow. "Thank you for agreeing to walk me down the aisle. I could have asked your dad, but this means more to me."

"I'm glad you asked me, as well."

Rylor led her down the hallway and out the garden doors to the flagstone patio that had been extended the entire length of the building. Trees, flowering plants, and grass had been trucked in from Fort Collins to complete the garden area in time for the wedding to take place.

Rylor had expanded the programs to be offered at the safe house and had kept the large barn exactly as it was. Horses had yet to be brought in, but those would come with time just as the workers would be selected in the coming weeks and days.

Rylor walked her slowly down the large aisle, smiling and nodding at the guests who had come out to celebrate the joyous occasion with them. Kaedon stood at the end of the aisle, smiling broadly as he bride drew nearer.

"Be happy, sweetie. You deserve it," Rylor murmured, kissing her cheek and then transferring the hand that had been on his forearm to Kaedon's. "She's all yours."

Rylor slipped back to a vacant seat next to Zane and watched as Kaedon and Jessie exchanged their vows. He couldn't help but feel a little left out as he watched both of his siblings enjoy being in the presence of their significant other.

Rylor had never had a serious relationship and he was ready

for one, he just needed to find time to find a girl.

"Excuse me, Mr. Ballard?"

Rylor turned upon hearing the soft voice and looked down into the greenest eyes he'd ever seen. The face was porcelain smooth and framed by dark red curls that hung loosely over her shoulders and down her back. She was dressed in a sweet top that left no observer in doubt as to her gender. She was short, maybe 5'4" tall and very petite.

"I'm sorry, have we met?" Rylor told her hoping the name was not one he recognized.

She held out her hand and Rylor took it, instantly feeling the sparks of electricity shoot up his arm. "My name is Melody Graham and I was told you might be looking for someone to head up your counseling department. I would like to be considered."

"Uhm… well, as you can see I'm not really in a position to do an interview right at the moment. Have you submitted your resume yet?"

Melody shook her head, "No, I prefer to do things in person. I'm staying in Warm Springs for a couple of days. Would it be possible to meet tomorrow or the day after?"

Rylor nodded, "I'm not sure of my schedule right now, but I would like to hear more about why you think your qualified for this position."

She smiled at him then and he felt all of the air leave his lungs. She was breathtaking and had a glow about her that couldn't be ignored and Rylor felt himself falling head over heels for a woman he knew nothing about.

She nodded and then walked away. He was still standing there staring after her when Tom came up and slapped him on the back, "Nice job."

Rylor looked at Tom in confusion, "What?"

"Getting her to talk to you. Nice. Several other guys have tried and she ignored all of their advances."

"She came to me. She wants a job here."

"Give her one and if you don't want to date her, I will," Tom told him with a laugh.

Rylor felt anger rise up and he tamped it back enough to issue a terse order. "No one approaches her but me."

Tom raised a brow at him and then shook his head. "You Ballard's are all falling into matrimonial bliss. I thought you were going to hold out, but no. Good luck," Tom told him with a clap on the back.

Rylor nodded and turned his head, searching for the red-haired angel once more. He didn't see her, but he didn't let that get him down. She was expecting him to contact her in the next day or two and he intended to do just that.

He did want what Jessica and Kaedon had found, he'd just like it with a little less drama involved. *Maybe now it's my turn.*

End

Sample of Book 3 in the series:

Book 3 title: The Heart Knows Where It Belongs

Prologue

Orlando, Florida

Six Weeks Earlier...

Melody Graham mentally counted to ten as she sat in the new clinical director's office, keeping her chin up and pasting a false smile on her face. The last fifteen minutes had seemed like hours as Bret had tried to explain how he'd come to be named the new clinical director of the Glenhurst Women's Center, even though Melody had been the one most qualified for the position. She had more tenure, more education, and more experience with abused women. She'd even met with several of the senior board members and had thought the position was hers if she wanted it. She'd never been more wrong!

"Melody, don't be a sore loser. Let's face it, this position really needs a man's touch," Bret told her in his sticky sweet voice that made her want to scrape her fingernails down a chalkboard. Bret was sitting behind the large desk in the director's office, dressed immaculately in a new suit to celebrate his new position, and the weak attempt he was making at growing a mustache made her want to laugh and offer him a tissue to wipe it off. "Let's face it, there's a big difference between listening to sob stories and managing an entire team of professionals."

Melody held her tongue, not giving him the reaction he was baiting her to give. Bret was a weasel and a poor example of a counselor. In her professional opinion, he was a narcissistic, male chauvinist who lacked the ability to empathize or show compassion unless there was a benefit to himself for doing so. In other words, he was a sleezeball who had no business trying to counsel women who had suffered horrific abuse at the hands of men.

Melody had always suspected that Bret was a fake and didn't really care about his patients, just the position and titles he might be able to obtain by appearing to be compassionate and concerned. He had confirmed her suspicions earlier in the week when she'd happened upon him speaking to a client in a most unprofessional and unbecoming way. The young woman had been so taken aback by Bret's demeanor that she'd fled the meeting in tears and it had taken Melody several hours to finally calm her down and undo the harm Bret has further inflicted on her fragile soul. She'd actually entertained the fantasy of calling him into accountability after being promoted, making sure he knew that type of behavior would no longer be tolerated. Well, that was a fantasy of epic proportions.

It seemed the board of directors had been swayed by his pretenses and in that moment, as she looked at him across the elegant desk, Melody had realized a harsh truth – she didn't want to have anything to do with a program run by people who were so blind and obtuse. Not getting this position was suddenly looking like a miracle and not devastating news.

"Bret, I'm sure you'll do a fine job. If I might offer one word of advice?" she asked in her trademark sweet and soft voice. Most of her friends knew that voice meant she'd had enough and was getting ready to set someone straight – politely, of course. Melody had been raised to be a lady at all times, even when soundly dressing down someone who needed it.

"Sure, you can offer. But you do realize that I'm under no obligation to follow it, right? I mean, I am the boss now. Speaking of which…"

Melody held up a finger and shook her head, "My advice? Remember?"

Bret nodded and rolled his eyes, "If you must share it, go ahead."

"I would keep the chauvinistic remarks to yourself from here on out. Ninety percent of our clientele are women who have been treated like pieces of property for most of their adult lives and some of them even have criminal records. A few of them would probably see a small stint in prison a small price to pay to shut the mouth of a pompous, self-righteous, fool like yourself."

Bret's mouth gaped, and Melody gave herself an imaginary pat on the back as she stood up. "It goes without saying that I quit. I have two weeks' vacation pay coming- I would strongly suggest you approve the request when it hits your desk. There's no telling what kind of damage I could do if I was forced to come back here and work for you."

"Melody! You can't just... well, I never..."

"And that's part of the problem, Bret. You've led a privileged life, never had to struggle or work for anything, and the thought of having to make a choice between medicine for your sick child or paying the heating bill has never crossed your mind."

Melody didn't wait to hear what else he might have to say. She stalked from his office and then forced her feet to slow down as she headed to clean out her desk. The eyes of the other counselors in the office sought hers and she simply gave them a small smile and nodded. She quickly grabbed the duffel bag she'd tucked in the bottom drawer for emergencies and started placing her personal affects in it.

She opened up her computer and quickly copied all of her personal files to a thumb drive before deleting them. The last item she grabbed from her desk was the letter from a friend she'd gone to college with. Inside the letter was an advertisement for a new safe house program starting up in Warm Springs, Wyoming – wherever that was. The advertisement wasn't of the normal variety and had been obtained because her friend had a connection to someone in the know. She was that kind of friend.

Sherry and Melody had been roommates her last two years of college and Sherry, better than anyone, knew that Melody longed to work with women who had lost everything and just wanted a chance to make a better life for themselves. The ad had been forwarded to Sherry and it had immediately caught her eye. Melody had to admit she'd been intrigued with the secrecy surrounding the new facility. There had been a name and a picture of a cabin, but no location. Sherry had gotten her the location, but only because her brother had been the one to forward the ad, knowing Melody and thinking she might be a good fit for the place. The facility was a *secret.*

Melody had even tried to research the facility online, but it was a ghost. No information was available, and it was as if the Freedom Ranch didn't even exist. Sherry had called the day after the letter had arrived and Melody had told her about her upcoming promotion and while intrigued, she'd denied any interest in contacting the ranch. Until today. Everything had changed and as Melody tucked the strap of the duffel bag over her shoulder and slipped out of the office via the side stairs, she decided it was as good a time as any for making a change in the way she had been living her life.

She enjoyed helping people, but working at the clinic came with all sorts of political games, insurance regulations, and a whole slew of public relations issues that simply impeded the work she felt called to do. An out of the way place hopefully wouldn't have so many restrictions, and as Melody had never even left Florida in her twenty-five years on this planet, she decided an adventure wouldn't be amiss.

It took her almost five weeks to get her affairs in order, to sell the things she didn't want to haul across the country, and to find someone to sublet her one-bedroom apartment. Bret had tried to call her several times, but she'd ignored his calls, just like she'd ignored all of the other calls she'd gotten from co-workers and even board members. She was done with this chapter of her life and ready to move on.

She told her sister and her parents she was making a change for the better. Her sister assured her she was going to love living in the mountains, as she currently lived in Denver, Colorado and worked for one of the big aerospace companies there. Her parents were on a humanitarian mission in the mountains of Mexico and wouldn't be returning until the school year was over. They had both expressed their support for her decision and told her they looked forward to visiting her in her new place of residence.

Melody promised to let everyone know as soon as she was settled, she loaded up her car and headed west. She'd thought about responding to the advertisement, but then decided this move was too important to be left to the U.S. Mail or an impersonal phone call. Not that there had been either option on the advertisement. There had only been an email address and Melody hated conducting business over the Internet. She was going to Warm Springs, Wyoming and she was going to convince the person in charge that she was the person for this job. Failure was not an option and she wasn't going to take "No" for an answer.

Chapter 1

Warm Springs, Wyoming

Middle of May...

Melody drove into Warm Springs with a smile on her face and expectation in her heart. She'd had a long, but very pleasant drive across the country, seeing things she'd only read about or observed online, and using the alone time to get her priorities straight once again. She hadn't realized how much compromise she'd been forced to accept while working at the clinic and she'd made herself a promise the night before that things were going be different this time.

She'd even gone so far as to list the things she wanted out of her life going forward: 1) a job where she truly felt she was being effective and helping people; 2) a community she could really become a part of, almost like a second family; 3) and love. Melody had always dreamed of meeting the man of her dreams, getting married and having a family, but so far, she hadn't even been in a semi-serious relationship. She'd dated a few times, blind dates and co-workers, but she'd never seen a reason to repeat the experience more than a few times with the same guy. She was picky and as her daddy had always told her, "Sweetheart, this is your future and you should be as picky and take as much time as you need to find the man God has set aside for you. Dating is a device used to find your soulmate. If you know after the first few minutes the guy you're eating dinner with isn't it, don't waste your time by agreeing to a second date. I promise you, he won't magically become the one during the second date and the propensity to lower your standards will increase with each subsequent date." Melody's dad was a wise man of God and she'd taken his advice to heart. Hence, she was very single and still looking for the place she belonged.

Melody drove down the main street, glancing at the clock on

her dashboard and frowning a bit at the time. It was currently midday, and there didn't seem to be a living sole on the streets. She pulled into the almost empty parking lot of the grocery store and her frown deepened when she saw the hand written "Closed for the Wedding" sign taped to the door.

"Wedding? Maybe that's where everyone is," she murmured to herself. She glanced around the rooftops and then spied the tall spire sticking up only a short distance away. She locked her vehicle and decided to walk in that direction, hopefully she would come across someone who could point her in the direction of Freedom Ranch.

She crossed the street, tucking her hands into the pockets of her lightweight jacket. There was still snow covering the tops of the mountains and a light breeze reminded her she was a long way from the ocean and the Florida sunshine. She inhaled deeply and then paused for a moment, thinking how clean the air was here. No salt. No tinge of exhaust. The sky was a brilliant blue, deeper than she'd ever before seen, and only a few fluffy clouds could be observed in the distance. She started walking again and smiled as the church came into view. It was small, but the parking lot and side streets were empty.

"Guess the wedding must be somewhere else," Melody told herself as she looked around, wondering what she should do now. Everywhere she looked, flower beds had been neatly tended and it appeared the occupants of Warm Springs took great pride in how their town looked.

She turned around and headed back to her car, noticing the sheriff's office was just a few buildings away. She headed there and was relieved when the doors opened when she pulled. She was anxious to find anyone who might be able to give her directions.

She stepped inside, holding still for a moment while her eyes adjusted to the dim light.

"Oh, hello," the woman told her politely. "Can I help you?"

Melody nodded and offered a smile, "Actually, I was looking for some directions. To the Freedom Ranch?"

The woman nodded, "If you were hoping to get there in time for the wedding, I'm afraid you've already missed the ceremony. The reception started a little bit ago, though, if you wanted to go up and extend your wishes to the bride and groom."

Melody nodded, deciding it was better to play along and get the directions she needed than let this person know she didn't know anyone in town. "That would be very helpful."

"Here, let me draw you a map," the woman offered, grabbing a blank sheet of paper and quickly drawing a sketch for her. "If you just follow the main road to the foot of the mountain and then take the first left once you start climbing, you'll arrive at the ranch before you know it."

Melody glanced at the sketch and smiled, "Thanks. I think I can find it now. My name is Melody, by the way."

"Sara Jane Plummer. I don't normally man the phones here, but I offered. I've been to enough wedding receptions to last a lifetime and it's not like I really need another piece of cake," the woman chuckled, indicating her very large figure.

"Well...," Melody paused, not quite sure how to respond. "I should probably get going or I'm going to miss everything. Thank you for the directions."

"You are very welcome. Could you give Rylor a message for me?"

"Rylor?" Melody questioned.

"Rylor owns the ranch and I promised him I'd come up tomorrow around 9 o'clock and help him clean up the garden area, but I forgot I have an appointment with Claire to get a haircut then.

Just tell him I'll be along as soon as I'm finished."

"Of course, I'll be happy to pass your message along." *And introduce myself at the same time. Rylor owns the ranch, so he's the man I need to speak with.*

Melody hurried back to her car and followed the street to the mountain and then headed up. She almost missed the first left turn, but she wasn't driving very fast as she couldn't quite stop looking at the landscape becoming visible to her. It was absolutely amazing and if she hadn't been convinced that she wanted this job before, she was now. She didn't know the people or how they did things in this town, but something inside her felt like she was finally... home. It was a feeling she didn't want to lose. Ever.

Thank You

Dear Reader,

Thank you for choosing to read my books out of the thousands that merit reading. I recognize that reading takes time and quietness, so I am grateful that you have designed your lives to allow for this enriching endeavor, whatever the book's title and subject.

Now more than ever before, Amazon reviews and Social Media play vital role in helping individuals make their reading choices. If any of my books have moved you, inspired you, or educated you, please share your reactions with others by posting an Amazon review as well as via email, Facebook, Twitter, Goodreads, -- or even old-fashioned face-to-face conversation! And when you receive my announcement of my new book, please pass it along. Thank you.

For updates about New Releases, as well as exclusive promotions, visit my website and sign up for the VIP mailing list. Click here to get started: www.morrisfenrisbooks.com

I invite you to visit my Facebook page often

facebook.com/AuthorMorrisFenris

where I post not only my news, but announcements of other authors' work.

For my portfolio of books on Amazon, please visit my Author Page:

Amazon USA:
amazon.com/author/morrisfenris

Amazon UK:
https://www.amazon.co.uk/Morris%20Fenris/e/B00FXLWKRC

You can also contact me by email:
authormorrisfenris@gmail.com

With profound gratitude, and with hope for your continued reading pleasure,

Morris Fenris
Author & Publisher

CPSIA information can be obtained
at www.ICGtesting.com
Printed in the USA
LVHW051531060421
683587LV00018B/224